Candy

Dish

MATTHEW LUTTON

This is a work of fiction. Names, characters, businesses, events, and incidents are the product of the author's imagination. Any resemblance to actual persons, living or dead, or actual events is purely coincidental.

Copyright © 2023 Matthew Lutton

All rights reserved.

ISBN: 9798858773108

Warning:

This book has terrible things in it. If you are not a fan of horror or violence this book is not for you. My books touch on subjects that are unsettling and might not qualify as "mainstream horror" however as I always say:

"If it makes you uncomfortable, its horror."

So turn back now or don't but if you get offended beyond this point it's your own fault or probably your father's but that's another book.

If you would like a bulk discount for book burnings, please contact me.

FORWARD

Written by Lisa Breanne

    Do you remember the day you met your best friend? Did you know right away that he/she would latch onto you like an octopus stuck to your face? Or was it a slow progression, (think Single White Female) where you thought they were oddly starting to resemble you more and more? Wearing your scent, listening to your favorite music, trying on your clothes, making sure you lotion regularly so they can make a flesh coat out of you……
I do, I remember everything…….

    What I thought would be a simple conversation with an author whose book I had recently read, turned into hundreds of texts exchanged, two-hour phone calls, video chats and now multiple trips to California and hours spent listening to and reading every word he has to say, with no end in sight. And to be perfectly honest, I don't know what I ever did without him. (You guys, I'm pretty sure he's drugging me).

    Most of you reading this, if any of you do, have purchased your minimum 10 drinks and your soul now belongs to Matt, it's why you're reading Candy Dish. Because like me, you've sworn your fealty. You will love these stories but you won't know why, you will consume them like the air you need to survive, Matt's word will penetrate you and you will take him wherever you go. You are his dolls, there is no escape.

Author's Note

You are reading something that wasn't supposed to exist. Writing a 2nd book was never an idea to be honest with you but alas dear reader here we are. So why are we here? Why did I write these stories? Well, you can thank (or blame) a certain number of people for the book you now gaze upon. I wrote *10 Drink Minimum* with the intention of it going nowhere and if it never did I left it open so fans could come up with their own endings and stories of the characters. If it got big maybe I would get published and get paid to write the 2nd one. If it got really big I would sell it and only want the merchandising because I love my characters like my own demented children. The 4th option (which I had not ever thought possible) was I would make friends from writing it. Now don't get me wrong I love money, but I am so thankful that fate landed on that 4th option. People started to read it and comments and praise were here and there. Some people actually started to recommend it to others. People I have never met before who owed me no obligation to share or praise my words (At least I don't think my mother could have paid them all to praise me) were offering to review my book and wanted to know when the next one came out. These people, who are acknowledged on the following page are the true authors of this book. I never plan to get rich from writing and the money I make off of these books is always a pleasure. There is nothing quite like creating something and having someone give me their hard earned money to (hopefully) enjoy it.

Now with that mushy shit out of the way I would like to address something right off the bat. This book is edited. If you have read my 1st book you will no doubt see the terrible editing that went into that book. I'm not making excuses but it is what it is. I was broke and after hiring 2 editors I put out the best book I could. People have asked if I'm going to re-edit it and my answer is no. Horror is special because its gritty and unpolished. I am not who I was when I wrote that book and it would be unjust to myself and the people who enjoyed and supported those stories to go back and take the "campfire" out of it. One review I read (not of my book surprisingly) said that while the story made sense and he enjoyed it very much the editing made it look amateur. I couldn't help but chuckle and I simply replied the truth: "But we are amateurs."

When you read my books I want you to get taken back to when you and your friends would tell each other scary stories. Back when you couldn't wait to see the expression on your friends face from a gross rumor or urban legend. This book, thanks to the very talented Amanda is polished and looks professional but I don't mind being Evil Dead over The Exorcist. These stories are here to make you think, laugh, appreciate and terrify you and I hope they do all of those things. I usually put easter eggs in my writing for fans to connect them to other stories or references to films or inspiration and I encourage everyone to message me the ones you find. I love interacting with everyone so please reach out. I want to thank everyone of you who has enjoyed something I've written and your continued support does not go unnoticed. You keep reading them and I'll keep writing them but just remember have fucking fun.

-Matt Lutton

Santa Ana CA Sat Aug 26, 2023

Dedication and Thanks (Most likely not you)

As stated earlier this book would not be possible without the help and love from many people. I will list them here but if I forgot any of you, I blame my old age.

This book is Dedicated to a certain group of individuals who helped promote me very early on. Without them this book would not exist:

Steph Stephanie

Amanda Jean Ruzsa

Lexie McDonough

Alexandra Russell

Kendra Raptor

Lisa Breanne

Mandee Quinn

Alyssa Cook

Kristine Prais

Special Thanks to:

My Mom Karen Lutton for being the strongest person I know and keeping the monsters away.

My wife Vanessa for supporting my writing from day one and bouncing back ideas with me about pumpkins.

My amazing friend and boss Daren who I have known since I was 18 for letting me be on my phone way more than I should be to promote.

My amazing friend Nikki for always being there and checking in.

Lisa for coming into my horror life and seeing something in me and my writing while sharing your vast wisdom and friendship with me. My amazing cover artist who didn't laugh at me and my cheap offer when I first started out Marcelle Silva

And finally, you for buying this book.

CONTENTS

Be Careful Out There	1
Can't Complain	8
Small Town	14
Gemini's Loveline	22
You Have Been Served	30
We the Clay	44
It's Just an S	48
Mind Yours	60
Don't Take Down Your Fence	66
Caduceus	75

"Christine, you must have been dreaming, stories like this can't come true. Christine, you're talking in riddles, and it's not like you!"

Andrew Lloyd Webber, The Phantom of the Opera

BE CAREFUL OUT THERE

Most people know nothing about cars. They use one every day and learn nothing from it. In fact, the average person spends 101 minutes driving per day. That's 37,935 hours if you start at age 17. I'm not judging; in fact, I never knew anything other than how to pump gas. I mean, I kind of knew how to check my oil, but I was no mechanic. I'm still no expert, but this job helps you pick up a couple of tricks here and there. It used to be just directions and movie times. Then we got bigger, with emergency response, and now we are at full-on vehicle diagnostics.

Most days are boring with the usual, "Good morning, sir! How may I assist you?" or "Your vehicle's temperature gauge seems to be on the high side. May I recommend getting it looked at?" or "The police are on the way to take your statement for the accident." Shit like that. The *most* exciting call I got was a freeway crash. A lady broke her leg. I tried talking to her, but she just kept breathing heavily and saying "ow" and "shit." Never anything tragic. Or bloody.

Most of the time we just play pranks on people. We'll roll windows up and down or randomly turn the volume up, full-blast. Maybe shut off an engine in the middle of rush hour. You find ways to entertain yourself and pass the time. All of our calls are recorded for customer service reviews.

The really nasty customers always want to talk to someone above you. Being on the other end of a phone line gives you some anonymity, so I usually put them on hold for a long time and make sure to keep the radio on Christian gospel at max volume, and then lock their car doors. They usually hang up; when they don't I pretend to be my supervisor, fire myself and then delete the call log. I genuinely *like* fucking with people. It makes the time go by. But what I really like about this job is the *power*. It feels pretty cool to know that I'm in control of over 100 vehicles at any given time. It's like having a train set, just on a much larger scale.

It's a Friday evening when I'm almost ready to leave for the day. I don't get out much, and I'm in no rush to leave, but still… I keep looking at my watch, debating if I should sneak out a little early. Then, a call comes in, ending the debate.

"Thank you for calling North-Star, how may I assist you, Mr. Boshcoe?" I ask.

"I need help!" The voice responding was so loud my ear immediately hurt. It was such a high-pitched sound I have to reprocess it in my head to confirm— with myself – that I'm speaking to a woman, not a creature.

"Ma'am, how may I help you?" I ask, holding the earphones off to the side like an itchy pair of earmuffs.

"He's gonna fucking kill me! I need cops!" The voice isn't any less high-pitched or any more pleasant.

I realize my employee number isn't officially logged with the network anymore, so the call is not being recorded. The shift change hasn't been adjusted with Daylight Savings Time taking effect recently. According to my monitor, I officially logged off an hour ago. I start to log back on for the recording process when her screaming stops me.

"I said I need the fucking cops! That fucking pig tried to eat me!"

I leaned closer to the monitor like that would somehow help me hear her better.

"I'm sorry, ma'am…were you attacked by an animal? Is that what you mean?" I asked, my question sounding like I was mocking her even though I wasn't. I was honestly curious.

"What...No! You dipshit! The John...the fucking owner of the car tried to eat me! FUCKING EAT ME! Chew me up with his fucking teeth! You hear me?" She didn't sound scared anymore, just annoyed.

I heard her. Oh, I *heard* her... and my entire being reacted. It was like seeing a plane heading straight for a mountain. Finally, something exciting. I needed this to be good. I needed this to last as long as possible. I looked around the quiet room, just me and a bunch of empty computer screens. Either my shift relief was very late or he wasn't coming.

"Hey fucko!" Her words snapped me out of my trance.

"I'm sorry, ma'am. I have alerted the police that you're in need of assistance; can you tell me what happened? I have you currently located in the mountains, near Shaver Lake, is that accurate?" I asked, working to sound panicked and not excited. Assertive, but not giddy.

"Yeah, the asshole has a cabin up here and he paid me for the whole weekend." She sounded parched, like a runner who had just finished a marathon with no hydration. She was a hooker. This whole situation was only getting better as the call went on.

"Okay, I'm gonna ask you to pull over. Officers have been dispatched to your location."

"I ain't fucking stopping," she laughed.

"Ma'am... Please pull the vehicle over so I can get assistance to you." I reiterated through gritted teeth.

"Look, kid... I almost just got eaten. And not in the way I usually get paid for, okay? So, I ain't fucking stopping until I see those Red and Blues."

I glanced around once more, ensuring my solitude as my hand hovered over the control panel. Satisfied I was alone, I entered the command code to disable the car's battery. The line switched to satellite, ending the call for roughly 30 seconds. Once my headset was restarted, I was again auditorily attacked by the angry cries of "Fuck" over and over. I could faintly hear the sound of the horn frantically beeping.

"Ma'am?" I attempted to shout over her obscenities.

"Fuck this, I'm calling the cops myself," she bellowed.

My fingers were tapping out the command codes before I even realized what I was doing.

I could hear her speaking to a voice I was unable to hear. "Yes? Hello! I need the…" The death-metal music at full volume I commanded drowned out any sentence she uttered. If she was screaming at the top of her lungs, neither the police, nor I, could hear her. I left the volume at max for a full 10 minutes, enjoying the music myself, then decided to engage with her again. Lowering the volume of the music I had forced into every inch of her vehicle; I could hear her breathing heavily on the other end of the line. She began to yell again and the impact alarm on my screen showed the driver's side window was being hit over and over. She was trying to break out.

"I don't recommend doing that," I said through the car's audio system.

"Mo-ther-fuck-er!" Her reply emphasized each syllable with hard kicks to the window.

"The vehicle you're currently occupying has been upgraded with impact-resistant race glass. The safety rating is quite impressive, actually."

She was still breathing hard but her voice was heavily annoyed. "What the fuck do you want, man? Money?"

I glanced up from the screen. *What did I want? Where was this going?* I had no grand plan. No end in sight. I answered her honestly.

"I just want to be God for a little while."

I don't think she appreciated my honesty because, seconds later, the impact alarm was sounding again. This time it was steadily increasing its frantic beeps, until suddenly it went dead silent, followed by a screech that echoed through my headphones. I switched the vehicle's dash cam on.

My little experiment was holding her right ankle at an awkward angle. The heel of her shoe had snapped, twisting it in a direction it was not supposed to travel. It was already turning purple, and her face resembled an Easter-egg-bowl of pain. Pink mascara slid down her cheeks to her flaring nostrils. The mascara and tears mixed with her snot to form a mustache that trickled into saliva, eventually forming a stalagmite of filth on her chin.

"I need... I need help... I need you to let me out of here." She said, looking around the car as you would look for God in the sky. Like a caring deity, I answered.

"I'm no Doctor, but that does look bad. Well, it's 32 degrees Fahrenheit outside. You are wearing what looks like a bathing suit? The nearest destination is a bait shop seven miles away...I have to say ma'am, this is not looking good."

"Please, please," she chanted over and over. My headset started to buzz when an alert on-screen showed the owner of the car was trying to contact us from his mobile phone. This was getting wild. It had turned from an experiment into a horror narrative. One that I controlled.

"Thank you for calling North-Star, how may I help you, Mr. Boshcoe?" I asked in my best customer service voice.

"Yes, my friend has borrowed my car and I need it back. Can you give me its location?"

I thought for a moment, then said, "That's the best you can come up with, huh?" Protocol was out the window as far as I was concerned.

"Excuse me?" he responded, sounding taken aback.

I started to type.

"Nothing. Look, the car, along with the hooker you tried to ingest as an appetizer, is 30 minutes from your location. I'm sending the coordinates to the BMW snowmobile that is in your garage at this very moment." I said dully.

The line was silent for a moment and then cracked to life, his voice oozing with confusion.

"What are you talking about? I..."

"Treat me like an idiot and I'll call the police."

He paused again. "Fair enough...Is the whore armed?" he asked, his voice now sounding more like what I assume CEOs sound like after exiting a press conference. Like an animal with its gag removed.

"No and she's injured, should be an easy hunt for you." I was about to click over to my subject when he asked why I was helping him.

I answered quickly and honestly.

"I'm bored."

5

I switched over to my injured little experiment. She was sobbing now.

"The police are on their way."

She laughed through her sobs.

"No, they aren't," she chuckled bitterly.

I turned the heater on full blast.

"Thank you," she whispered. I smiled.

"Of course. We don't want you going into shock. There is a first-aid kit in the trunk. Can you get to it?" I asked.

"I don't want to move," she said.

I blasted the radio, then cut it off just as fast, to jolt her.

"I didn't ask you what you wanted to do."

She started to cry again.

"There is a road flare in the kit. Your monster is about fifty feet from your location. Good luck." I unlocked the doors. She had a choice to make. Fight or flight… well, fight or crawl, in her case. I sat back and waited. She hesitated, calculating her decisions.

She tried to lock the doors, but they unlocked as soon as she tried. She screamed and crawled to the back seat, each movement drawing forth more agony. But she was determined. I leaned closer; we could hear the snowmobile approaching now.

"Twenty feet away now, better hurry," I said, the crunch of boots and a humanesque oink accompanying each footfall. Each oink grew louder with every heavy step.

"Fuck," she said through gritted teeth. "Shit, shit, shit, c'mon!"

She was in the trunk now, frantically searching for a weapon or the first-aid kit that I had promised was waiting for her.

"Oh, shoot. The model of the vehicle you're in stopped carrying first aid kits two years ago. They moved them underneath the passenger seat, for easier access… funny, huh?"

The lord giveth and the lord taketh away. Boschoe ripped open the driver-side door, slid into the vehicle and closed it behind him. He was wearing a mask that looked to be made of discarded doll hair and rotting pig skin. He was completely nude except for his heavy, old boots. In his meaty paw he clutched a knife. I locked the doors and leaned into the microphone once more.

"Give me a show," I breathed.

He lunged for her, doing things that you only heard of in shocked, whispered circles. After about an hour of mayhem, he asked me to turn the air conditioning on or crack a window. He was covered in filth and gore, almost as though he had gutted an elk without removing the correct parts first. I put the AC on full blast.

"That's a little too cold." He grunted, wiping himself down with the tattered scraps of clothing previously worn by the deceased little experiment.

When he started to visibly shiver, he yelled, "Hey, turn the fucking heat on!"

I leaned into the mic.

"Hypothermia sets in at 35 degrees. I will turn the heat on one minute after that, don't worry." He stopped cleaning himself, his hand frozen on his chest mid-wipe as he frantically looked at the locks on the doors. He then looked around at the beautiful trap I had led him to. He understood what was happening now, and he was terrified. He pulled off his mask and peered into the dashcam.

"Tell me what you want. Money? Girls? To keep watching? Name it!"

I leaned in just as close as he did.

"I just want to be God for a while."

Can't Complain

Ben liked this Starbucks the most because they rarely messed up his order. It was simple with few ingredients.

"Iced Caramel Macchiato, upside down, please." Ben smiled and showed his rewards app to the young, plucky barista.

"You're always in such a good mood," she said, smiling back at him.

"Hey, I can't complain," he said, picking up his drink from the counter and waving goodbye. He had a busy day ahead of him, but luckily the funeral home was only a couple blocks away. As he walked through the big, winged gates and into the somber office, a young lady greeted him.

"Good morning. I'm Rick Ellis, Debra Ellis's son." Ben extended his hand, and the young lady took it, shaking it softly. "Of course. I'm very sorry for your loss, Mr. Ellis."

Ben nodded and gripped her hand. "That's very kind of you. I came over because I know my mother has been dealing with the proceedings, but we all decided that my dad should be cremated rather than buried."

The young lady's lips formed a tight line. "I see. Well, we can arrange for that. However, we would need Mrs. Ellis to…"

Ben feigned a worried expression. "Oh, no, please, my mother is mourning and I'm afraid that any more of this talk would have her in there right next to my dad. I understand how this puts pressure on you all. Since we have already paid for the funeral, the family and I agreed we would like your business to have whatever is left over. As a token of gratitude for handling our father with such grace. And leaving our mother to grieve."

The young lady's face went from concerned to incredulous in an instant. "Mr. Ellis, Sir, that's way too generous."

Ben took her hand in his and put his other hand on her shoulder. "Please, call me Rick. Mr. Ellis was my father." Ben said, his voice cracking, seemingly on the verge of spilling tears. The young lady handed him a tissue and Ben handed her a twenty-dollar bill.

"You're very kind. Please call my mother and tell her when it's done." The young lady nodded, and Ben wiped away his tears as he exited through the slow-closing doors.

Ben walked towards the pet store a little over 20 minutes away and sipped his macchiato while fidgeting with the loose coins and pieces of paper in his left pocket. As he finally neared the pet store entrance, he excavated the crumpled receipts and newspaper clippings, chuckling to himself as he tossed the freshest one with the headline proclaiming, "Man of incredible faith, Joseph Ellis, dead at age 78, to be laid to rest in Olive Tree Jewish cemetery."

Through the double doors, the smell of smoked meat and dog fur filled Ben's nostrils as he made his way down the aisles of multicolored dog toys and rows of fish living out their boring existence to the sound of lights humming and filters swirling. He finally arrived at the cages in the back. Here, displayed for all to see, were the worst of the catch– like a freakshow hidden at the back of the county fair. No adorable puppies or cute kittens competed for attention here; only the abused and abandoned lay, most shivering, on display.

"Breaks your heart, don't it?" The middle-aged, balding clerk said, tapping the glass in front of Ben where a poodle with no right ear, eye, nor teeth acknowledged the men's existence with a perked left ear, then sank back down into his mundane existence. "This one the most fucked up?" Ben asked, not breaking the sad thing's stare. The man eyed Ben, trying to come up with some professional way of answering, until he finally sighed and simply stated, "Yeah, someone fucked her up bad."

Ben and the dog walked out the doors and towards the bus stop, just catching the doors as they were about to close. The bus driver looked at Ben and then at the Dog. "No animals unless it's a service dog." Ben and the mutt looked at each other until Ben motioned for the dog to walk up the steps. "I'm taking him to get put down, can you please look the other way?" The bus driver looked at the dog and back at Ben. "What's wrong with him?" she said with an almost disgusted expression.

"He got hit by a bus," Ben said, appearing to stare right through the driver, nearly making her shiver as she waved them both on. The bus had the usual crowd of students, hobos, nurses, and the elderly. Ben sat behind a housekeeper crossing off her grocery list and checking off bills. He could make out the list since it was written in a form of "Spanglish." Everything was checked off with neat little red check marks except "Deposit Rent." Two envelopes lay at the bottom of the woman's pink purse and as the bus neared the animal hospital Ben stepped down hard on the dog's tail making it yelp and bark loudly, startling everyone as they followed the dog with their eyes to the front of the bus. Ben grabbed the envelopes from the purse and made his way with the dog out the door.

"Put that fucking thing out of its misery," the driver yelled before she pulled the door shut and drove off. Ben took the cash from the envelopes and pocketed it while walking into the lobby. He sat down, petting the dog as it bobbed its head while taking in all the new smells. The woman next to him seemed nervous.

"Are you alright?" Ben asked, stroking the dog's course and dirty fur. The older woman smiled and stopped chewing on her nails to scratch behind the dog's ear.

"It's my Taffy– my cat, her name is Taffy and she's real sick and the bills just keep coming." Ben nodded his head, then said, "I know how you feel. Rusty here has cost me over 50 thousand! But I love the little guy."

"Stephanie," the woman said, extending a hand for Ben to shake. He took her hand gently and told her his name.

"What happened to Taffy?" He asked, still holding Stephanie's hand.

"I found her as a kitten. She had so many fleas it took all night in the bath to kill them. Her and I have been through a lot together and she was my daughter's favorite before she passed away. I feel like if anything happened to her, I'd lose the last part of my daughter I have left." Ben nodded and let her hand go while Stephanie looked down, embarrassed. "I'm sorry, that was a lot."

"It's fine, really," Ben said, patting her hand.

"She has cancer and the chemo treatments and the surgery…"

Ben pulled out the cash from his pocket. "How much is Taffy's treatment?" he asked while counting the bills. Stephanie eyed the cash and then shook her head, holding up her hand in protest.

"No! No! I couldn't," she protested, on the verge of tears.

"How much," he said, plainly, sounding almost annoyed. Stephanie quickly composed herself and thought hard.

"His surgery will be ten thousand dollars," she said, after running the numbers over in her head until she was satisfied it was the correct amount. Ben stopped counting and looked her in the eyes.

"I don't have that much on me, but I will take care of it. You just tell reception I'll be taking care of everything from now on." Stephanie was about to protest, but Ben simply held up his hand with $1,000.00 in it. "Go get Taffy a bunch of new toys. And a new bed for her to heal on when she gets home."

Stephanie was crying now. Her smile was so wide it resembled a PEZ dispenser. She took the money and hugged Ben so tight he almost had to push her away to let his breath out.

"You're an angel," she said, squeezing his hand.

"Don't tell anyone." He winked and they both chuckled.

"Now, go tell the front desk I'll take care of Taffy," Ben said, shooing her away. Stephanie kissed his cheek and walked to the front desk, then pointed to Ben before signing some documents. They waved Ben over and he handed them one of many fake IDs he kept with him while on his "outings." Stephanie hugged Ben one more time as the receptionist entered all the information into the computer.

Soon, Stephanie was waving goodbye to Ben and the dog. After a few minutes, Ben took the dog with him to the parking lot of the McDonalds across the street and tied his leash to the door. Ben called his favorite hotline and reported various sightings of missing persons, each of which he made sure were at least two states away from their last known location listed in the paper. The operators hung up the phone sounding more appreciative and hopeful after each call. With the day winding down, Ben decided he would only make one more business call on the walk for his evening Frappuccino. The music on the phone wasn't as annoying as he thought it would be, with new radio hits actually keeping him entertained until the receptionist came on the line. "Reeser's Emergency Animal Hospital," the cheery voice said, sounding well-rehearsed.

"Evening, I'm calling on behalf of Taffy and his course of treatment."

The line was silent for a moment, then, "Oh, yes, she's a very good girl. She seems to be responding to the treatments!" The receptionist exclaimed, sounding genuinely hopeful.

"Yes, our little guy is happy and has no pain for now, which is why Stephanie and I have decided it's the right time to avoid any further pain or suffering." The line was silent again.

"Are you sure that's the best…"

Ben cut her off, saying, "As you know, we have already spent a large amount of money and we don't want to risk our baby being in any more pain, especially when we can't afford it anymore."

Soon, the receptionist began typing. "I understand." Her tone was all business now, some training kicking in, Ben was sure, about not letting emotions get to them.

"When would you like to say your goodbyes?" Ben shifted the phone to his ear while he opened the door to his Starbucks.

"We already have this afternoon, and my friend would like to be contacted as soon as Taffy passes to set up the pick-up." More typing was heard, and then her voice got louder as the receptionist moved closer to the phone.

"The Doctor will be helping Taffy's transition in 30 minutes. You will be able to pick him up tonight or tomorrow, whatever is easier for you both."

Ben smiled. "I will leave that up to Stephanie. I appreciate your time and thank you for taking care of Taffy." Ben mouthed "Java Chip" to his other favorite barista, and as he made the fake gun symbol to his head, they both laughed.

"Ok, we will proceed then, and contact you as soon as it is done. Have a good night." The nurse waited in silence until Ben broke from his teasing with the barista over this 'horrid work call' and said, "and you as well, thank you."

Ben sighed, putting the phone in his pocket, then sipping on the blended goodness to end his day. The barista laughed as Ben turned and walked towards the door. "We all want to know how you stay so positive!"

Ben stopped at the door and smiled, a wide smile. "Well, someone always has it worse, right," he said, and with a nod in agreement, the barista waved goodnight.

Small Town

Tucked away near-Death Valley lies the small town of Brenbook, Nevada. It is a small town and, until last year, its population had been decreasing by roughly 20 to 30 citizens yearly. While this is not strange in and of itself, the reason for the yearly exodus is. You see, the town of Brenbook no longer celebrates Halloween. In fact, any sale of Halloween masks has been outlawed by the town's acting Sheriff, John (Redacted), who has become very popular amongst the Brenbook residents ever since. I met with Sheriff John in person and, after some off-the-record negotiating, he agreed to speak to me.

The following interviews have been obtained with permission from the Steven Blak YouTube channel. They are available unedited on said channel. Steven: Sheriff, I want to thank you for agreeing to speak with me and my viewers as we look at the weird and wacky around the world. Sheriff John: Yep.

SB: Sherriff, I love Halloween! It's a big reason I became a paranormal researcher! It blows my mind that a whole town doesn't celebrate Halloween. I mean, I could never live here.

SJ: I'm sure I speak for the whole town when I say thank God for that.

SB: Sheriff *and* comedian! So, tell me… why don't you like Halloween?

SJ: Halloween is an excuse to commit crime. People dress up and hide behind masks to cause…chaos. I won't stand for it.

SB: I get it. I mean we've all had our house toilet-papered or had a bag of flaming shit stamped out on our porch, but is that enough to ban a beloved holiday?

SJ: You sound like my predecessors.

SB: They sound like smart men.

SJ: They don't sound like anything anymore. They're dead.

SB: Uh-oh, well I hope you didn't kill 'em, huh?

(Sheriff John remains silent)

SB: *Did* you kill them?

SJ: I told you I won't make this town a laughingstock. We have been through too much to be told we are crazy again.

SB: My viewers are very open-minded. Please.

SJ: About four years ago we used to be a very festive town in October. This town's heat levels are ridiculous. We hit the hundreds daily, but people love to have a reason to dress up and celebrate. We had the usual witches, skeletons, clowns and whatever superhero was popular that year, but we also had a new mask popping up. A simple white paper plate. With two eye-slits and a red smile, and with twine holding it on the head.

SB: That doesn't sound so bad.

SJ: No, it doesn't, does it? Maybe that's why as the day went on and more and more people were brandishing the same simple plate mask, none of us really noticed until I got home and saw a package with no return address on it. I took it inside and told my daughter how cute she looked in her princess costume, and told my wife how hot she looked in her kitty costume.

(The sheriff stares off in the distance.)

SB: Sheriff?

SJ: Sorry. I looked the box over, no marks, no writing, just tied together with simple packing twine. Inside were three paper-plate masks. One for each of us, I gathered.

SB: Who sent it?

SJ: For a guy with a show, you don't listen well. I don't know.

SB: Did you put it on?

SJ: Eventually.

SB: Okay, so somebody sent you some creepy masks, I don't see cause for alarm. Maybe somebody was trying to get you in the Halloween spirit.

SJ: Everyone.

SB: Huh?

SJ: The whole town.

SB: I don't follow.

SJ: The whole town got a package. Each containing the number of masks equal to the number in the household.

End.

☾☾☾

The sheriff refused to answer any more questions, so I went looking for more info on these packages. The postmaster refused to speak to me, claiming that no packages were delivered by her mail carriers unless it had proper postage on it. Brenbook unfortunately does not have a library, so I was at the mercy of the local tavern patrons. Against the advice of my wife and camera crew, I approached every patron, even the more unsettling looking ones. I was told by a biker-looking gentleman that he would use my skull as a urinal. A homeless-looking man eating pancakes just kept laughing and chewing away, occasionally taking swigs of syrup, as we hurried past him to the bartender, who pointed us towards Amanda (Redacted).

SB: So, you also received a package on Halloween four years ago?

A: No, I mean, yes, but we get them every year.

SB: You get a package of masks every year?

(Amanda looks nervous and around at the bar.)

A: I don't think we're supposed to talk about it.

SB: I have permission from the Sheriff.

A: He never talks about it. I used to babysit Nicole.

SB: Who's Nicole? His daughter?

A: Yeah. She was nine.

SB: She passed away?

A: No, well, yes. She was killed. I mean, everyone was.

SB: Wait, who killed her?

A: The masks. The people in the masks.

End.

☙☙☙

At this point, we were told to leave the bar by a group of angry patrons. I told Amanda we were staying at the local hotel and to please come find me.

We were woken by a knock at the door and a very angry Sheriff. He pushed me onto the bed, his revolver pressed against my cheek, cold and oily. My wife was screaming, hitting him and screaming at him to get off me until he relented his grip and holstered his gun. He told us we weren't welcome here anymore and that this town had been through enough. I tried to calm him down, but he walked to his car and came back in with a plain box, tied together with packing twine and placed it on the bed beside him.

The following is also captured on a tape recording I obtained without the Sheriff's permission.

"You assholes are stirring everything up. I had it contained. It was gone for a whole year, it was gone and now you come up here and…"

The sheriff begins to weep, unholstering his pistol.

"I put the mask on to scare my girls. I went upstairs and my wife was posing in the mirror. I don't… I didn't mean to hurt her, but I had never felt so angry in my life. I wasn't mad at *her*, but at *everything* and *everyone*. I felt every problem I had ever had bubble up to the surface and my rage was boiling over. I only felt better when I felt my wife stop breathing, and my muscles relaxed from squeezing her neck so hard. My daughter was tugging at my shirt, and I saw a red smile staring at me. She must have grabbed one out of the box. We held hands and walked out into the yard, watching the chaos unfold around us as people in *those masks* committed terrible acts on those without them. We felt like we were in an alternate reality and it was us against them. So simple. By the time the sun came up, we were both covered in blood. We threw the masks off and held each other, crying with many of my neighbors, coworkers and even church officials, all doing the same. The FBI came in and arrested all of us, many of whom turned ourselves in. We all were told mass hysteria and herd mentality were to blame. Just a tragedy, with no one to burn at the stake and no one to blame. We all did time. Until the next Halloween. Until the packages showed up again. Stories were told around town, sure, but you hear shit like that and 4 out of 10 people are gonna call bullshit, especially if they are young and stupid. We had 106 homicides that Halloween. The FBI came in this time, blaming copycats, until a bunch of psychiatrists cleared almost everyone for no homicidal signs or tendencies. The government kept it quiet and ran tests on our drinking water and anything else you could think of. Finally, they let us all out and they sent a team for the next year. Just to make sure everything goes smoothly."

The Sheriff laughs hard, his sobs going in and out of joy and agony.

"The fucking idiots just made it worse. The toll for *that* Halloween was 209, with 20 government agents dead, and my daughter hung from a tree, but you won't find that on any government record. They sealed us off, labeled us all as crazy and haven't returned our calls. The media won't answer us. You're the closest thing to a reporter we've spoken to, and we don't have any historical records of the town. Hell, I'm only the Sheriff because I took the position after stabbing the former one in self-defense. So, I gathered what was left of us at the church. I told everyone that no mask would ever be worn in this town again. That Halloween could go back to hell where it came from and that year, we didn't get any packages. No mask was seen, and we all acted like life was normal. Then today, I saw this on my porch."

He nudged the package with his gun.

"Do you know what day it is? You would be surprised how easy it is to forget the day or even the month. Most people wouldn't even know it was Christmas without the lights and the trees and the goddamn Santa Clauses on everything. I don't need to open it. I already know there's one in there and I want to put it on. I can feel it calling to me like a glass of water to a thirsty mouth, or a fire to a shivering animal. I won't do it…Happy Halloween."

The sheriff then shot himself, spraying his brains against the hotel wall. After calling 9-11 and only getting a busy signal I decided to cover the Sheriff with the bed sheets. My wife, as I write this, is cussing me out and saying we should get the fuck out of here, but I won't let this hysteria affect us. If something is here, I'm going to get it on film for you guys…. so, please, hit that like button and stay tuned.

❂❂❂

The following testimony is presented for educational purposes only. No sources could be verified at the time of this recording due to Mr. Blak's mental state.
Officer: It is October 31st, just past 3:04 a.m. I am with Steven Blak who has declined his right to counsel and wishes to speak with me freely.
Officer 2: This is a bad idea, the guy can't even put a sentence together.
O1: You a fucking lawyer now? Shut up.
O2: Whatever, I'm going to get coffee.
O1: So, Steven, why did you kill your wife?
S: Masks. Was the masks. Everywhere. Calling.
O1: Steven, we found you in a cave wearing this stupid fucking thing covered in bloody handprints.
S: Get it away from me! Get it away!
Shuffling noises with more screaming.
O1: Steven, you knock that shit off! I want to know what you're doing on my side of the county and why your wife was found eviscerated near my town!
S: Leave. We tried to leave. Tried to get out to the next town. I took the box, needed proof, nobody would believe me without proof.
O1: I don't believe you, so make me believe, Steven, tell me what happened. Were you coming from that fucking leper colony over in Brenbrook?

19

S: We left the hotel. We fought, but the rooms. They all had boxes. All the rooms had boxes outside.

O1: Steven, I don't give a shit about boxes and if you don't start making sense I'm gonna stick you in a box for the rest of your life, you get me?

S: We got in the car and drove, but it was too late. They were everywhere. A lady dove on our hood with her baby, begging us to take it… I just drove faster. I had to swerve to not hit people in the street. They were killing them out in the street, wherever they caught them… they just killed them like it was taking out the trash or grabbing the mail.

O1: So, you had accomplices? How long have you been planning this, Steven?

S: No planning. Impulse just… go go go. Makes you feel things. Angry.

O1: Why did you kill your wife, Steven?

S: Scared. I was so scared… we hit something. Made the car slow. Masks surrounded us, started banging. They broke the back windshield and started to crawl in. I didn't have a choice. Only had one.

O1: You only had one what, Steven?

S: Mask…the sheriff's. I told her how sorry I was, and I slipped it on. Then I saw it. I saw what they all saw.

O1: What did you see, Steven? What the fuck are you clowns doing? I'm in the middle of an interrogation! Take those stupid things off!

The tape ends after a scuffle is heard with what is presumed as officer number one gagging.

The town of Brenbrook is abandoned and has been deemed a no-man's-land by the federal government due to 'previously unnoticed levels of radiation.'

The Death Valley Ghost Murders has been the number-one paranormal video on YouTube since its upload. It is periodically taken down and reuploaded. The neighboring town of Weightfell, Nevada has denied any knowledge of ever having Steven Blak in custody and deems the audio tapes a sick joke. Coincidentally, they have enacted a new city ordinance of no Halloween decorations or masks to be worn in town during October.

When asked for comment, the mayor declined.

Gemini's Loveline

"Don't you love me?" Jason looked up at Jenna like he was a puppy begging to be loved enough to be adopted.

"You know I do." Jenna sighed for what seemed like the thousandth time; they often had this particular sparring match that led to her needing to prove her affection. She placed her arms around Jason's neck, bending down to kiss his lips and look him in the eyes. He wrapped his hands around her waist, pulling her close, so his face was between her breasts. She laughed and pushed him back as he smiled and slid his hands down to the bottom of her ass, inching closer to her crotch. She pushed the hand away playfully and it was his turn to sigh in frustration.

"Three years, Jen." He held up three fingers, like it somehow made the statement more damning.

"I mean, everyone else? Three months, maybe! But years? Hell, I'm pretty sure half the guys on the team have already had sex more times in the past three months than we'll *ever* have at this point."

Jason threw his hands up, then let them fall to his sides on the bed, giving up.

"I'm not *like* everyone else, Jason," Jenna said, matter of fact but with a hint of sadness.

Jason looked down at his chest. "Not what I meant, Jen." He pushed his hand through his blonde curls and blew out a long sigh. "I don't know, maybe it's me. Maybe you're just not as serious about me as I am about you."

Jenna held his cheeks in her hands and kissed him, licking his lips and planting a small kiss after each lick, like a little signature on a love note.

"I love you. Hey, I *love* you, okay," she said, making him look her in the eyes. "I'm just scared, okay? It has nothing to do with you or us or how I feel about you."

Jason rolled his eyes. "Then what is it? What is there to be scared of? You're on the pill! I'll wear a condom... hell, I'll wear five condoms!"

Jenna giggled, imagining Jason trying to look sexy as he ripped the condom open and placed it on his cock, then repeated the process four more times while trying to keep the mood going.

"You're so romantic," Jenna teased, clutching an invisible pair of pearls around her neck.

"I know. I am irresistible," he teased back, striking a pose with his chin in the air.

"But seriously, talk to me, what are you afraid of?"

Jenna sat down next to him and fidgeted with the cuts on her middle finger. "Look, you know my brother is super protective of me."

Throwing his hands up, Jason cut her off. "Jesus, him again? I've never even *met* this asshole! He can't be *too* scary if he's never around!"

Jason stood up and paced from one side of the room to the other.

"Seriously Jen, how would he even know! He's not going to bust in and catch us! He hasn't caught us together yet, right?"

Jenna nodded, but then shook her head, saying, "That's different"

Jason threw his arms up, dropping them to his sides once more, making Jenna wince at the sound of his hands smacking his sides.

"How? *How* is it different?"

She didn't say anything, only looked at her hands in her lap.

"Okay." Jason said, deep in thought while he placed his hands on each hip. In an 'aha' movement, Jason threw a finger up in revelation.

"What about a hotel? Huh? He would never know! Nobody would ever know, we'll go to the next town over," he said, nodding with each word, confident he had solved their problem.

"My family…" Jenna looked down, ashamed. "My family is… different. We have certain values, and we don't have sex before marriage, but…" Her look turned from shame to hunger, and she moved in close to his chest, kissing his neck while unbuttoning his pants. Any argument Jason had left to make didn't seem important anymore. He lay back on the bed and welcomed Jenna's mouth. He gripped her hair and controlled the speed of her lips as they traced his cock.

"Do that thing I like," he said, moaning the words. Jenna stopped sucking, but stroked him while she spoke.

"You know the deal. I get embarrassed, so you can't watch," she said, teasing the head of his cock with her hand.

Jason sighed with pleasure. "But I'm already watching babe, c'mon."

Jenna stroked slower, but harder, making Jason shudder.

"Nooope." She stretched the word out as she shook her head.

Jason gave up protesting and grabbed the bandana he kept tied around his lamp. He gave her one last look, then tied it tight around his eyes, waiting for her to inspect it as always. Jenna gave it a couple tugs, and then after rubbing his chest some more, Jason felt the tip of her tongue inch the head of his cock. He never could understand how she controlled it the way she did, but it felt amazing, and she always finished him off by licking with the tiny tip inside his pee hole. It was always a better orgasm than the last and he didn't understand why he wasn't allowed to watch her while she did it. But, whatever her terms, they were worth it.

The last year of high school flew by and while Jason may have inched himself closer to taking Jenna's virginity, she never relented in her stance of being married first. Jason thought about leaving, about going after someone easier, but he loved Jenna and eventually, he proposed.

Jenna stared at the ring and pulled Jason up from his knee.

"Is that a yes?" Jason asked nervously, looking around at the crowd watching anxiously.

"If we do this, you have to promise me that you will love me." Jenna sounded serious, like a lawyer explaining a contract.

"Uh yeah, I kind of figured that was part of the deal." Jason smiled, motioning to the ring still waiting in its box. Jenna reached for it but stopped her hand before removing the ring.

"Love me *and* my family," she stared into Jason's eyes.

"I promise," Jason said, nodding and smiling.

Jenna took the ring and slipped it onto her finger, then kissed Jason on the lips quickly, almost like she was signing a contract as fast as she could.

The night before the wedding, Jason and Jenna had a lovely dinner and talked about how excited they were. Until Jason asked the question that had been on his mind all day.

"So, do I finally get to meet him? Ya know, get his approval?" Jason teased.

"Meet who?" Jenna asked, mouth full of desert, which she was devouring since she had been on a diet for two months to fit into her wedding dress.

"Your brother, silly," Jason said, stealing a bite of her cake.

Jenna put her fork down and slowed her chewing.

"He's away, out of town," she said looking at the mess of frosting and vanilla ice cream on her plate that had looked neat and tidy when first brought to the table.

"He's going to miss your wedding? I thought you guys were close?" Jason sounded angrier than he meant to.

"You'll meet him. He just can't come to the wedding. I'd rather not talk about it, I'm nervous enough as it is," she said, finally meeting his eyes and matching his tone.

"You're not getting cold feet, are you?" Jason took her hand in his and smiled, trying to lighten the mood. He did not want to start off his marriage in a fight.

"It's not that," she said, pulling her hand away and brushing her hair back in frustration.

"Talk to me. 'Cause if you can't tonight…" he trailed off, but they both understood what he meant. She grabbed his hand and looked at him, trying to reassure him.

"Look, my brother and I are close and who *I* love, *he* loves. Trust me, he is going to adore you. He already does."

"He's never even met me, how would he adore me? For two years this guy has blocked us from being together and the day that we're finally going to be married, he's not even going to show up?"

"So, are you marrying me just to fuck me?" Jenna's eyes narrowed, almost closing completely.

"NO! You know what I mean." Jason began back-pedaling as fast as he could, "If it was just sex, I could go out and…" Jenna's eyes went wide, like a camera shutter opening.

"No, no, that's not what I meant, hold on." Jason pleaded, but Jenna was already grabbing her things and walking towards the door.

"Do not follow me." She held up a finger to stop him. "I will see you tomorrow," she said, walking through the heavy wooden doors of the restaurant.

"Or I won't," she yelled over her shoulder in a flippant tone as the doors swung shut.

Jason didn't sleep well at all that night. He tossed and turned, thinking of how stupid he had sounded at dinner and what he would say to make it up to her. *That is, if she showed up*, he thought as he finally fell asleep.

The next day at the church, Jason was relieved when Jenna's bridesmaids told him she was upstairs getting ready. Waiting at the altar, all of his doubts and worries dissipated at the sight of Jenna in her dress. As he held her hand and helped her up the steps to join him in the journey to marital bliss, he started to spill all of the things that he thought would excuse last night's debacle, but she held her hand to his lips and looked directly into his worried eyes.

"Me *and* my family, you swear?" She was almost pleading with him. Jason nodded and brought her hand down from his lips, then grasped it tightly as they both smiled.

In the hotel room that evening, Jenna seemed more nervous than she had at the wedding. Jason poured her a glass of champagne and she emptied it instantly. He laughed and filled it again, trying to reassure her that she had nothing to be nervous about.

"Sweetie, it's okay. We will go slow," he said, pulling her close and brushing the hair from her face. Her shoulders loosened and she seemed to relax, or at least stop fighting what was making her nervous. He went to touch her, down there, finally… but she held his hand as it entered her panties.

"Let me start, okay?" Jenna said, standing up and tugging Jason's boxers down. Then she was pulling his cock deep into her throat before he could object. Jason moaned and laid back on the bed, letting his muscles relax.

"Close your eyes," Jenna said between strokes and licks. Jason looked down at her and protested, but she stroked harder. "Please," she said again. He nodded and covered his eyes with his hands. The pleasure stopped, and then seconds later the tip of her tongue was working the fold around his cock like a tattoo-needle of pleasure. Finally flicking the inside of his pee-hole, she brought him to the edge until he couldn't take it anymore.

"Babe, I'm going to cum, stop, I want to be inside you."

Jason lifted his hands from his eyes to see Jenna standing before him; her face was an expression of unease and dread, her shoulders slumped, almost bracing for physical impact. Her beautiful, perky breasts were still, not moving their usual cadence with her respirations. Jenna held her breath out of fear and her smooth stomach tightened, creating a trail of visibly contracted muscles down to her clean shaven… Jason froze from fear, the way you would when seeing a rattlesnake. There was nothing he could do but stand as still as possible and hope this was a nightmare.

At the top of Jenna's vaginal lips, a small abdomen protruded and connected to it were two tiny, useless arms, like a fleshy t-rex. Worst of all, atop it was a tiny head, whose milky-white eyes were staring at Jason's cock while its tiny tongue licked the tip of his penis like a hungry little dog. Jason wanted to vomit, scream and cum all at once and he dared to look away from the monstrosity, only for a second, searching Jenna's eyes for something, anything, that would save his sanity from this moment. Jenna crossed her arms like a person trying to shield themselves from the cold and looked at Jason, ashamed.

"Jason, meet my brother."

You Have Been Served

Sam looked around the room. It was late, around 10:00 p.m. People were enjoying their drinks; the alcohol was good and it was clean. They were drinking and laughing and more enticing than those, they were all eating. Sam looked down at her plate and tried to fight back the nausea. Tonight was a big step. At least, it was to her therapist of six years. She had told her that nothing bad was going to happen. She told her that nothing bad was *in* or *on* her food. This was a new restaurant. They didn't know her here. Sam cut into the plain, unseasoned chicken breast; well done, just as she had instructed. She used her fork to hold the meat in place while she tried to saw through the toughened hide, then brought the piece up to her face for inspection. It looked innocent enough. No pink. No black dots. No unknown liquids. She put the fork down and breathed in, just as they had discussed in her second therapy session of the day. She lifted the fork and smelled the morsel. The odor seemed off, it always did. She called over her waiter and stuck the fork in his face.

"Smell this."

The young man laughed until he realized she was serious. He did as he was told and smiled. "Smells great...is there a problem ma'am?"

She didn't answer except for the shooing motion she gave him with a pale, wrinkled hand.

Up came the fork again, but this time she dared to bring it to her lips. It was a mistake that she instantly regretted, and her body responded as it always did to this miscalculation. The vomit came out in slow gurgles, almost like a baby spitting up. Sam had gotten good at keeping the retching noise to a whisper level, but she couldn't help the face she made that resembled a stroke victim. Nor could she hide the bile and acid from the daily dose of vitamins she needed to keep her body nourished. She wiped the green and white liquid from her lips and looked around. People were still laughing, but they weren't eating anymore, and they weren't drinking. Some looked concerned, but most were repulsed and disgusted. She felt the same way she did every night for the past six years... like a freak.

Sam gathered her belongings and began to walk to the door, right past her waiter. She could feel the cold air of night that comes with being near the beach as she pushed the door open. She was almost outside when she heard her name. The nausea was building again. She closed the door and turned back to the waiter.

"What the fuck did you just say to me?" She screamed. The young man looked terrified, like a boy hearing his parents yell out his full name in anger.

"Uhhh, have a good night, Ms. Smith, and I hope you feel better," he said, thinking she had just misunderstood him and this would buy her forgiveness.

He was wrong.

She advanced to him, yelling every word that made people feel small. She was enraged, assumed he was in on *it*... just like they all had been for six long years. Six years of no sleep. Six years of malnutrition and six years of hospitals, both medical and mental.

The waiter went home that night and laughed it off with his friends, that crazy lady.

Sam Smith, however, went home and hooked her IV tube up to her wrinkled, emaciated arm and cried.

The next morning, she filled a glass fresh from the dishwasher with water from her Brita filter. She started the usual ritual of running it through the filter, as she did every morning. After the 28th filter cycle, three hours later, something close to comfort crept into her and she sipped the drink. She took small sips, always, tasting it and swishing it to make sure nobody had contaminated it.

Sam sat on her oversized couch and looked at the pictures on the wall. Her kids didn't visit anymore. She watched her grandchildren grow up on Facebook walls and scrolling through albums. She sent gifts and called, but they were ashamed of her. They never told her to her face, but she could tell they, too, thought she was crazy. She didn't care what the test results said and she didn't care how crazy what she had said sounded. She knew the truth. She was being poisoned. Maybe not with arsenic or any other fatal ingredient, but poisons all have the same intent and purpose.

It started six years ago at the grocery store. She had lived in the area and shopped at the three local stores for years. The kids had grown up on food from the store and celebrated parties and graduations with treats from its bakery. She had trusted them. Trusted them enough to feed their food to herself and to her children. One night after dinner, she felt sick and diarrhea soon followed the stomach ache. The girls had felt fine. Perhaps their younger immune systems fought off whatever was ailing her. She shrugged it off and the next day was like any other. She met with her lawyer to go over her latest lawsuit, but the whole time her stomach was uneasy. She eventually went home and slept it off. A couple nights later there was a celebration, and the cake was just as she had ordered. It was moist and delicious, however that queasy feeling followed her relentlessly. She emptied the trash into the bin and rolled it to the garage where she saw a single envelope sitting on her driveway. She had always thought the mailman was competent at his job until that moment, and she retrieved the letter and sat it on the kitchen counter. It was white, the size of a piece of paper and smelled of bleach. She was cautious, but her curiosity won over her fear. She looked it over. No markings, no name, no address. It probably wasn't even for her. She ripped it open and pulled out a post-it note with one sentence written on it.

Enjoy the cake.

She smiled and set it down. It must have fallen off the cake, perhaps a note from the baker. She went to bed that night with her stomach still storming. In the morning, her children woke her up, saying they both had bad stomach aches and wanted to stay home from school. She was hesitant but agreed before changing into a jogging outfit to go get a cup of coffee. On her way back to the house, she came to an abrupt stop just before her home. In the middle of her driveway was another envelope. She was annoyed now. Customer service be damned, this was ridiculous. She set her coffee down and opened the envelope to find several photographs within. She stared at it for a long time, going over the images in her head. This was weird and she could not register that the picture showed a pair of gloved hands holding a giant, filthy rat. The rat was covered in what appeared to be either sewage or some type of grease. The next picture was even more odd; it showed the rat being placed in a bowl of what might be some type of mud. The next one showed the rat walking on and digging in the sludge. She was flipping through the pictures like a bestseller now. The pictures became a flip book of the rat chewing and gnawing at the mud but then the reveal of the last picture made her freeze. She couldn't speak, she couldn't move. The picture showed the rat being rewarded with a piece of cheese. The orange of the cheese stood out against the yellow that it was placed on. The words *Enjoy the cake* visible on the post-it note the rat and cheese were perched on.

  The phone calls and letters that followed were like bullets from a gun, gift cards and apology letter after apology letter were delivered (none ever admitting guilt), but after a while her fury had diminished, and life went back to normal. Occasionally, a flu bug would catch her, or a headache would keep her from a meeting. Her lawsuits were failing because of her absences. After a meeting at a popular restaurant she had decided to invest some money into, her head started to ache. She was tired; she knew this, but the pain kept nagging at her. On her way home she decided to stop by her Doctor's Office as he was a friend from the club, and she was due for a visit anyway.

  She was expecting a Tylenol, at most a Vicodin, and then she would be out of there. But that wasn't the case.

  "Have you been out of the country at all, Sam?" Dr. Jacob looked concerned, and he rarely didn't have a smile on his face. He was not smiling now.

"No, I've been much too busy. I have a lot of court dates around this time every month." She mused, trying to bring a hint of a smile back from him, more for her sake than his own.

"Hm. You eat anything weird or undercooked lately?" He opened her file and sifted through it.

"Is something wrong?" It was her turn to lose her smile.

"Cysticercosis."

He said the condition matter of fact, like she should know what it means.

"What the fuck is that? Cancer?" Sam squirmed.

He was shaking his head before she finished the question. "Tapeworm. You have a tapeworm."

Sam laughed, then said, "I do not have a fucking tapeworm." She reached for her coat from the chair. She wasn't cold, it just seemed like the thing to do to emphasize the offensive nature of the words he had just spoken to her.

"Well according to the bloodwork and the scan, you do have one and you have had one for a good while, judging by the size of it. About four months, I'd say," he said it gleefully, almost as though he enjoyed her challenging him. He handed her the black and white picture and circled the long tube-like line that was coiled in her stomach. Sam immediately felt the saliva build in her mouth and she rushed to the sink, emptying what little substance her stomach held into it.

"It's alright, I'll have a nurse clean that up. I'm going to write you a prescription. Make sure you finish the whole regiment and check back with me in a week."

Sam never went back. She did finish the prescription he had given her and after a long, embarrassing week she passed the small serpent that had been hitching a ride in her guts. It floated in the toilet, dead and surrounded by the red of the medication. She flushed the toilet and took the hottest shower she had ever taken in her life.

The next couple months were hell. She would sanitize her fruit to the point of not being able to eat them. Her hands had become blistered and raw from the soap and alcohol she sprayed and lathered them with whenever she touched something.

They looked old, older than they should look, especially with the money she spent on manicures.

Her children tried to make her stop but they didn't understand; someone was watching, somebody was always messing with her food somehow. From long hairs to fingernails to God knows what. She complained, she wrote reviews, people were starting to talk and some even had the gall to accuse her of placing the things in her food herself. She still had the status her money could afford her, but in a rich town like this, she was becoming more trouble than she was worth, and she was worth a lot. She had done everything she could. She switched grocery stores, traveled to other cities to have dinner. And still, she *always* felt sick, ranging from feeling slightly uneasy to full-on bloody diarrhea. She had scans done and had taken every test imaginable. No poison and no severe stomach damage. Her doctors eventually stopped taking her calls. When her children had moved out of the house and told her they would stop talking to her if she didn't get help, she had finally gone to see her therapist. Her diagnoses were Obsessive Compulsive Disorder, Anxiety and her therapist felt she maybe had a bit of Germaphobia.

Not a single person believed her but she knew what was happening; she could see it in their false greetings and condescending smiles. Every "welcome" and "great choice" was venom dripping from the host or waiter's lips, just waiting to be mixed with her food somehow. The chicken fiasco last night was the final straw. Pretty soon she would have to be fortified intravenously if she couldn't start eating.

The doorbell ripped her from her thoughts. She didn't want to answer. She had no makeup on, and her vanity was on par with her hunger pains. The bell sounded again. It was an ominous thing now that she thought about it. Ding Dong… Ding Dong… a melancholic little melody each time. She had thought it cute when she had bought the house; now it made her uneasy. She stood too quickly, she realized as she walked towards the large door. She was dizzy, and her slippers clacked on the wood as she stumbled more than walked, catching her pale light frame on the door. The damned doorbell rang *again*. She breathed in deeply, letting the chime end, and on the final 'dong' she flung open the door.

A man stood on her step. He was short, a little muscular. He wore all black with a purple tie. He had horrible tattoos on his arm, little black things that looked like bats. His beard was combed but you could tell this wasn't always the case. It looked like a cross between a Viking and a hobo.

He smiled at her. "Morning, Ma'am."

Sam's instinct to slam the door almost got the better of her, but she looked him up and down and curiosity changed her mind.

"What can I do for you." It wasn't a question, it was a statement. It held the same meaning as "Have a good day, Sir," when you told off an employee. What it really meant was "Go Fuck yourself."

The man's grin grew wider. His teeth were yellow, stained with what looked like years of constant coffee consumption. He didn't smoke, she could tell from the scent of him, although he looked like a smoker.

"Actually, Ma'am, this conversation is more about what *I* can offer *you*. May I come in?"

Sam was shutting the door before she had even finished saying 'no thank you,' but his big, black boot made the door stop and quiver in her hands, startling her. She was annoyed now and looked up from the boot to his now-serious face.

"You have my word... I will not touch you, but I believe that I can help you with your..."

It was his turn to look her up and down. "Food allergies." He said, winking at her.

Sam's stomach dropped and her grip eased up on the door, letting it swing open wider. The man nodded as she motioned towards the couch. He sat, then leaned forward and put his elbows on his knees. His eyes followed her, watching her move from the door to the big wooden chair in front of him. It was an uncomfortable, wooden monstrosity that had been hand-carved in Italy. She used it whenever she was meeting someone who wanted an investment from her. It made her look intimidating. This man, however, did not look intimidated at all. Instead, he was smiling again. No, not a smile... a smirk. Like a chess player who knew he was about to win and there was no stopping it.

Sam broke the silence. "I would offer you some Tea or Coffee..." she said, letting the words dissipate in the air.

"And yet you have not."

"Coffee or Tea is what you offer a guest...You...are not a guest. So, what do you want?"

The man smiled wider now, showing his teeth as he pointed at her. "All business. I should have expected that," he said, leaning back into the couch "I appreciate it. However, I don't think I have the time to wait for you to strain it 28 times like you normally do."

He was smirking again. Sam's stomach hurt more than usual, the nausea mixed with despair forming a cold thunderstorm in the pit of her belly. *How did he know that? How could he know that?*

"I don't know..." she started to say as he quickly stood and started to pace from one side of the couch to the other.

"You do, though. You know very well what I mean." He pulled his hand from his pocket, producing a piece of hard candy and unwrapping it. He let the wrapper float to the floor mid-pace and popped the bright red thing in his mouth. Sam was about to protest but he spoke over her.

"Did you know I write stories? Of course, you don't, we haven't met. Not officially. I want to tell you one I think you will like."

Sam looked at him and scoffed, then said, "Okay, I..."

He interrupted her, again, "Good, I'm glad you agree. Imagine, if you will, that you are rich." He winked at her. "And you go around town like any rich person would, looking for ways to turn that one million into two million. Now, nothing wrong with that, that's the American dream. But this rich person..." He pointed at her as he continued, "That's you, remember. Imagine this rich person goes to many bars and many restaurants in town making business deals. You start to be recognized upon sight; they have your tables ready for you and they know your drinks, your food preferences. It's good. It's nice. it's easy."

He was talking too fast for her to get a word in.

"Let's say one day one of those business deals go south." His smirk abruptly turns into a sad face, then quickly back to the smirk. He's moving the candy around in his mouth, playing with it as he talks, tapping against his teeth with it.

"One of the business partners drops dead, it happens, unfortunately, but now the investment doesn't work out how everyone thought it would. Now, you're very rich, but you didn't get rich making bad investments, so you decide to sue. You speak of how you were lied to, these people came to you and made you promises they knew they could never keep. You were just the victim, you have no choice but to try and get your money back. Well, unfortunately nobody has the money you want so you go after the next best thing. You go after the people's property; you go after their families."

Sam had heard enough. She stood up and opened her mouth to throw the man out, but he stopped pacing and stared at her, his smirk gone. He interrupted her again, but he was quieter now, not excited, but calm.

"Sit… Down." It was a threat, not an order and not a request. Sam swallowed and straightened her jacket, then she sat and looked at him, trying her hardest to not appear the least bit intimidated. She could tell it wasn't working. He resumed pacing again, not looking at her while he talked, which made it even more uncomfortable.

"Now, the wife of the dead business partner, she is hit with all kinds of shit. So much shit that the fan breaks with how much has been dumped onto it."

His tone changed. Sam could tell there was a deep anger there, maybe even sadness. It frightened her. She glanced around for something she could use in case this got… *unpleasant*. "Your lawyers harass her. Send her threats disguised as fancy legal documents; they are all very business, very professional, but the widow sees them for what they are. Every letter that says "Lean on your property" reads as "Homeless" to the widow. These words haunt her, replacing her grief with fear. They keep her up at night like a boogeyman tapping on her forehead and whispering, every hour on the hour."

The man jumped onto the sturdy wooden table designed to look antique and lurched toward her, his face an inch from hers. He roughly tapped his forehead.

"Homeless," he whispered through gritted teeth, jabbing his finger into the center of his furrowed brow.

"Fraud," he tapped again.

"Alone," he tapped again.

"Dead," he tapped.

"Broke," he tapped.

His skin was protesting in little cuts getting redder with each tap.

"Walmart Greeter." he kept tapping.

"Liar." Tap.

"How could you not know?" Tap.

"What will you leave your children with?" Tap.

"At least three more years." Tap.

Sam was crying now. She didn't know what this was or where it was going. She whispered, "Stop." She watched the blood drip down his forehead, down the bridge of his nose and into his beard.

He smiled, exposing blood-coated teeth, then chuckled, resembling a hyena after a kill. He raised his blood-stained finger and slowly tapped her forehead. He looked at her with no anger, no sadness, no emotion at all. He simply said, "No." He jumped off the table landing with a thud on the wood floor. Sam wiped her face quickly, the way a mouse cleans itself, ridding her cheeks of her tears, moving the blood from her face into her hands and filling the small lines that age and stress had created over the years.

"I don't know what ..." She started to say as calmly and quietly as possible; she didn't want to rattle him, but he interrupted anyway.

"So, the children get together. They think of ways they can save their mother from this monster that torments her so. However, none of them have the financial means to fight back and sadly they are all at a loss. They are all hard working. Even though they came from privilege, they had all started work young. Surprisingly, they had all landed in the service industry. They were all well-liked in these businesses of Food, Beverage and Hospitality; which was nice, but didn't really help them much in this situation."

Sam was listening, but she also just wanted this to be over. She knew it would not end well, but at least he would be gone and she would be safe. So, she sat and she played her part as his audience. Finally, he sat down and pulled a piece of paper out of his pocket. He placed the heavy inkwell pen that adorned the wood table onto the thin sheet of paper and then unwrapped another piece of candy, discarding the wrapper onto her pristine floor, not taking his eyes off her the entire time.

"Now, I want you to pay good attention because we are coming to the end of our story," he said, pushing the new, yellow piece of candy halfway out of his mouth as he spoke. "The human body can go up to 21 days without food. The human body is amazing and 21 days without food is excruciating, but it is survivable."

He reached into his pocket and pulled out a purple, wrapped candy and slammed it onto the table. He was looking at it like a child gazing at a Christmas present trying to guess its contents. Then his eyes shifted to hers.

"Just because you *can* survive something doesn't mean you *want* to." He picked up the purple candy now, rolling it around in his hand. "You see, everything is tracked nowadays so it only makes sense that this information would be stored somewhere. Your favorite foods, your favorite drinks, what your husband likes on his toast in the morning… all these wonderful algorithms taking little bits of you and storing them. Making your life easier and the restaurant and grocery stores' jobs easier. This way the baker knows that your six-year old's birthday is coming up and they can send you an email reminding you how much her and her friends enjoyed last year's cake with the chocolate icing. Or, how the bartender knows how you like your whiskey poured. You give all this information away to complete strangers. People who handle your cars, your hotel rooms, your cellphones and, of course…your food."

Sam's stomach felt like she had swallowed ice.

"Now, this information still has its safeguards. Laws are in place and it is kept secure so not everyone can access it. However…" The man starts to unwrap the candy on one side. "There is a rumor of a 'black book' so to speak. Now, this book, you see… it's not an *actual* book; it's more of a living, breathing contract among Hosts, Servers, Cooks, Valets and the like. Let's say somebody leaves a five-dollar tip on a thousand-dollar invoice from the Ritz. That person's name gets passed around and, of course, in such a tight-knit industry everyone knows them from one restaurant to the next. Now, rumor is… it used to be you would write down the name, the offense and then a number. One meant not so bad, maybe don't refill the drinks at the table every chance you get… but a 10 … if someone saw your name and a 10 was next to it— in a smoking area scrawled in chalk behind a dumpster or on a cocktail napkin passed to a bartender. Well…"

Sam still felt nauseous, but she had stopped crying now. She didn't know whether to cry again or laugh. She had been right. She *wasn't* crazy.

The man started to unwrap the other side of the candy. "Well eventually people started getting into trouble. Too many complaints and writing things down… well that just leads to getting caught. So, an honor system was introduced. Purely word of mouth. You would give a name and a number, and the bounty would be placed. If you were found to have lied about the offense, *your* name went on the list, so nobody dared make up a false claim. Now, most people think 'well, nobody would mess with somebody else's food on rumors' and most of the time you would be right, but if you have ever worked in a retail job…which, well, I'm sure you haven't. There is an "all for one and one for all" attitude when it comes to service workers: An offense against *one* is an offense against *all*. Not to mention, you can't be *everywhere* the person whose name you put on the list goes; you must take care of *any* people on the list, and you are to rest assured that somebody is doing the same for you somewhere." He put the candy into his mouth and smiled. "Did you know that you can eat gallons of semen and not get sick? It's mostly made up of water." Sam's stomach seemed to be talking to her in sensations, responding to his words. Like a psychological test of 'tell me the first word that pops into your mind' only instead of Sam's mind … it was Sam's insides.

Q: Urine?
A: Pain
Q: Fecal Matter?
A: Nausea
Q: Semen?

A: Vomit

Q: Pubic hair?

A: Coughing

Q: Snot?

A: More Nausea

Sam wasn't listening anymore, but her stomach was and, finally, it physically shouted in protest. Murky water erupted from her mouth and emptied onto her shirt. She was a mess, covered in a mixture of tears, blood, bile and vomit.

The man laughed. He laughed so hard his mouth launched the piece of candy onto the table. It slid all the way across, gliding through the pool of her vomit like a tiny ice skater, stopping just before falling over her side of the table.

She wiped her mouth and smiled. "I'll have you arrested. I'll bury you. Do you hear me? I will leave you so poor that you will be living on the fucking street, and then I will buy the street... the one that you are sleeping in your own shit on, and keep buying until you have nowhere to fucking go." Her confidence was coming back now.

He stood and straightened himself. "You could do that. However, these are just rumors and once you're on the list you can only be taken off the list by the person who put you on it... and that, well, that takes years.... or that's how the rumor goes anyways." He smiled.

Sam was not used to being in a position like this. She was completely helpless.

"I'll pay you. I'll give you whatever you want, but I need it to stop. I need to get off this list and get my family back. She jumped up and ran to the kitchen, grabbed her checkbook and rushed back to the gore-covered chair and plopped down in a mess of her own filth. She grabbed the pen and looked up at the man.

"What's your name? I'll write it right now, just tell me a number."

He walked over to her, his face close to hers. He picked up the vomit-covered candy, its purplish color leaving it to look like a melted candle of sick. And through her gritted teeth, he pushed it hard into her mouth.

"You know my name."

She was biting him, but the candy stopped her from piercing his finger too deep. He didn't seem to mind, didn't even seem to notice. He yanked his fingers out and wiped them on her mess of a coat.

"Every time you eat you will remember my name. You will remember what you did and each chew that tastes like something is off, each little too-sweet or too-sour spoonful of soup, you will see my face and you will remember that you fucked with the *wrong* family."

Sam began to cry again, and soon, she sobbed. She was on her knees, begging, pleading with him. He just kept smiling.

"I'll make you a deal," he said.

Sam was nodding furiously.

"You see, I think there is a hit here. This little story of mine. However, I don't have the startup capital."

It was Sam's turn to interrupt. "Anything, any amount, just name it," she said, tugging at his pants and effectively dousing his boots with the sick dripping from her face.

"This is a two-part deal. You will call your lawyer and tell him you're starting a publishing business. That you want to make good on some past mistakes. And that I have pitched my story to you, and you think it will be a hit. You're so confident that you have paid me an advance of ten million dollars and made me a partner."

Sam was nodding as she wrote the check, then spit the filth-covered candy from her mouth as if to solidify the signature. The check hung in the air, her arm reaching out like a person falling off a cliff–reaching for his hand to take hers. Save her.

"The second part," he said, sitting down and ignoring the furious shaking of Sam's still-raised arm with the check.

He reached across the table and grabbed the pen, then placed it gently on the piece of paper he had pulled out of his pocket earlier. He pushed it toward her, avoiding the river of sick that had now started to congeal on the old wood.

"This is for you to write how *you* see fit. Only rule is no mention of me, except that you want to make it right with me and that you are sorry."

The realization of what he meant hit Sam like no wave of nausea ever could. "Forget it... no," she leaned back in the chair and dropped the hand with the check to her lap. She eyed the pen and piece of paper like it was a snake coiled and ready to strike her.

"This is not a request," the man said as he began cleaning the blood from his face as best he could, but it wasn't working well.

"I will not do that. I won't. I need to be with my girls again. I need to live again... get out... get out and... and..." Sam knew she was backed into a corner.

The man looked at her. He was almost sympathetic looking. "Turn the paper over." He said it with a tinge of regret in his voice.

She looked at him and then to the paper. She grabbed it lightly like it would cut her if she held it at the wrong angle. She slowly flipped it over, then dropped it as if it had bit her. But then quickly grabbed it, holding it tight, hiding it from anyone seeing it, anyone grabbing it, anyone knowing of its existence. "No, no, no, no. You wouldn't. You *can't*," she pleaded.

He looked at her and she realized she had seen this face a thousand times before. It was a strictly-business mask. It was the face of tearing down a family-owned restaurant to build a parking lot. It was the face of raising the rent in low-income-housing buildings. It was the face of "this is just business, it's not personal," and he simply mouthed the words, "I would."

The man got up and walked over to grab the check from her defeated grasp. "There's a gift coming for you before you go. You have my word, nobody has touched it."

The doorbell rang its melancholic tune. He crossed the room and opened the door, mumbled a few words and then turned around to place a giant pizza box on the messy table. The smell was orgasmic. Sam looked at it like she should be praying to it, not looking to devour it like a wild animal. He started to walk away but she grabbed his hand.

"You promise...this...this is clean?" she asked, like a mother begging for a child's life.

He grabbed her hand and looked at her, said, "On my father's grave," then patted her arm and walked out the door.

That night, after Sam had cleaned up and washed the sickness from her furniture, she made the phone calls she needed to make. The man would get his ten million. She wrote her letter. It was long and it told her daughters how much she loved them. How she was sorry for everything she had done wrong in her life and that they would be better off without her. She then ate every piece of the pizza the giant box held. It was the most delicious, most desired meal she had ever had, as well as her last.

She emptied the bottle of sleeping pills into her hand, reflecting on how completely full she finally felt. She tucked herself into bed and swallowed the handful in one, big gulp. As she slowly started to drift off to sleep, the bottle fell from her hand and onto the bed, then rolled and dropped into the wastebasket next to the note the man had pulled out of his pocket. It sat there, an empty bottle now, simply stating the facts of its now-emptied contents; just another discarded thing with words that meant nothing to anyone anymore, just like the note with the names of Sam's granddaughters written on them… and a 10 written next to each one.

We The Clay

"Let the official record show that Chairman Lute has cast his vote of *YAY* and would like it noted that this is a waste of time."

The cacophony of voices was drowned out by the banging of the Prime One's gavel as the council finally retreats and settles to mumbling; collectively, they glare down at the accused. The man in the lone chair is chained at the feet and wrists, his hair is dirty and dreadlocked, and his beard is only slightly cleaner.

"Does the accused have a defense he wishes to declare?"

The man in the chair raises his head. His face is aged and tired, but youthful and beautiful, changing like ripples in a lake. He gazes at each of the eight persons seated about him.

"What wouldst thou have me say?"

"Objection, let the record show we will be hearing testimony and sentencing in the simple speak as it is commonly known in our systems," shouted the Prime One, seated in the highest chair between the others, his voice booming for all to hear.

The chained man speaks once more. "Fine, what would you like to hear?"

The council shifts in their seats, each one of them wanting a different reaction from the man... begging, crying, remorse, fear; the list goes on.

"We are here to decide what to do with you and your abomination before it grows beyond our control," the Prime One announces.

"It was never under your control... I see now that it was never under *my* control."

The hubris of both parties gives way to fear as the last statement settles in the air of the large chamber.

"Be that as it may," the Prime One says through new resolve and gritted teeth. "It and they are now our responsibility. I, for one, would like to know what made you abandon protocol and act as though you had the authority to create such a creature?"

The man in chains thinks for a moment, in silence, and then a smile crosses his cascading features. "At first, it was because I could. Move this here. And watch how this grows. Take this away and see what fails, what thrives. Cause and reaction. It's what we all create for."

The Council's faces are a mixture of dissatisfaction, amusement, and understanding.

"We are not here because you decided to create. That is our purpose. It is in our nature. We are here to understand *why you continued*. Even after we have ordered you to cease and destroy this... this *cancer*. You allow it to *thrive*. I want to know. *We* want to know. Why?"

The chained-main's expression changes from a smile to a scowl as he mutters something under his breath.

"Speak up!" The Prime One's voice fills the room again, growing darker.

"I said 'because you told me I couldn't,'" the accused one says matter-of-factly. Murmurs erupt in the chamber until the Prime One silences them with a question. "It is that simple, is it? You were told no, so you did?"

The man stands, his chains rattling as he shifts before speaking. "Nothing with *them* has ever been simple. Trust me. They are the greatest mistake I have ever made. And yet, also my greatest accomplishment."

The sound of scoffs and chuckles quickly becomes deafening in the echoing ground chamber.

"Accomplishments? Yes, they have many accomplishments, don't they? The extinction of five billion different species in only 200,000 sun rotations. Over 15 million enslaved. And 46% of the natural fauna decimated. They are masterfully adept at destruction."

The Prime One exhales and composes himself as best he can, but the outrage is still swirling in his eyes.

"They…" The chained man is interrupted, the Prime One's voice growing icier.

"You yourself ordered the destruction of them at one time. We had thought you sensible then. Until we heard of your little side project."

The man bows his head in acceptance of the statement. "I wanted to try another way. I saw… I *see* potential in them." He lifts his head to expose a single tear gliding down his cheek, his features shifting like broken static.

"We also see the potential they have. The potential to destroy and infect other universes. They have already claimed one planet. Luckily, it is an uninhabited planet. But now they have sent machines to another! We cannot allow your cancer to spread."

The council members all nod in agreement.

"They need more time. They are still young. They have faults. They have made mistakes. Terrible mistakes. But they have also created. They have loved and shown us wonders. They have created symphonies that have even stirred emotions in me. I beg of you, give them more time."

The Council looks to one another. The Prime One is visibly quaking; his fist tightens as he speaks. "Music."

The word hangs in the air.

"Your defense is that they create music?"

"They…"

"Hold your fucking tongue or I'll have it removed," the Prime One interjects. "We have microorganisms that produce music, creatures that sing simply for amusement. And none of them have destroyed at the rate of your *humans*. You have created this virus and even after failure, time and time again, you let them continue. It is clear you have forgotten your place. You believe that you *are* this God they claim you to be. Well, it is time for judgment, and unlike you, I will be just and swift with it."

The chained God begins to shout in languages of its own creation, its form shifting from places known as Egypt to Europe and so on. Its face changes to the many versions its creation has given him.

"It is my and the council's judgment that you be locked in the void where no sparks of creation can be conjured. You will remain there until we all join you in nothing at the end. The planet, known as Earth, will be cut off from any other system. And... no life shall be permitted to leave it, henceforth."

Two giant men entered the chamber and escorted the God-in-chains to his eternal prison. His protesting cries voiced in all human languages echoed throughout the chamber and down the hall, until silence settled among the eight still seated.

"You made the right decision."

It is not clear to the Prime One's ears who said it, but it is quickly repeated among his peers.

"Destruction of the planet known as Earth shall now commence. Proceed."

The windows of the ship slide upward. The stars filling the dimly lit hall resemble little fireflies in the now-doomed planet's forest. The eight look upon the green and blue ball, and with a few strokes of a keypad, the planet folds in on itself until nothing but stars fill their view. The eight nod to each other and leave, one by one, with only the Prime One looking out amongst the stars, then nodding to the task that was done.

Over the years, tales of 'the humans' and 'Earth' spread across the stars. Legends were born, histories were studied, and cults gathered in worship of the late species. All in all, most of the races lived in harmony. Science thrived on creating disease. On most planets, it is obsolete. However, with no conflict, the minds of the brightest scientists (who now called the former moon of Earth home) stumbled across a peculiar looking package. Upon further testing of the vials labeled *SpaceX*, the chief scientist decided that bringing a species back from extinction was well within scientific guidelines, and he would only be making two of them - one male and one female - how much damage could two beings cause?

In the distance, where no light and no sound has ever been seen or heard, laughter echoes across eternity.

It's Just An S

The machines are a cacophony of beeps and pings with the sound filling every inch of the small hospital room. My eyes are fluttering as men in black suits drag in screens, then box my bed in. Three clicks lock each screen together, leaving only a small opening. A man places a chair next to my bed before helping an older gentleman settle into it. The final click seals the box, leaving just the two of us. The older man places his wrinkled hand on top of mine, gently, and I realize it's David. He's older now as, I guess, I am too. It doesn't matter, it won't be long now; I can feel it. David smiles, patting my hand as he removes his hat, then says, "Lexie, we need your help. You have to make him stop." He says it plainly, not pleading like the men before him. I smile. At least I think I do. My face went numb about an hour ago.

"It's not funny, Lex," he says, answering that unspoken question. "He's killed three senators, destroyed our largest oil pipeline and torn the head off the leader of Mexico's biggest drug cartel. On *live* television."

We stare at each other, neither of us giving away anything to the other. This is how we argue, it's how we have always argued. A war of tells. I break the staring contest by looking towards what should be my window but instead, I am greeted by a lead-lined, portable wall.

"What makes... you think... I could stop him?" The words are tough to get out as my throat is dry.

"You're his mother. He loves you, he trusts you," David implores. It would sound sweet, admirable even, if you didn't know the purpose behind it.

"Just like you wanted him to?"

David frowns as the venom in my words wounds him. I almost apologize.

"That's not exactly fair, Lex. I have always supported you and Christopher when you needed *anything*," he said in defense.

I scoffed; even he didn't believe that. While it was true he had helped clean up some... incidents, he was never there like he should have been. In fact, he had only started referring to Christopher by name around his ninth birthday.

"Father of the year." Four words that I knew would destroy him. It was a dirty move, but I didn't have much time left anyway.

David leaned in, his face serious and stern. "Let's not start comparing parenting techniques now. It's a little late for that when your boy is destroying government property left and right. If anyone's a failure here, it's you, Lex,"

I smiled, taking the criticism. I was 39 years old when I was given the mission and now, at 82, I have done my best to raise my son to be what this world *needs*.

SSS

I had arrived at the fertility clinic early, like I was asked to do the day before. "6 a.m. sharp," the nurse on the phone had said, and that it was *very* important I was not late. The office was filled with women, all around my age, white, slim and relatively fit. I was told by a lady behind the nurse's desk, one who I had never seen before, to wait until I was called; then the Doctor would come speak to me. One by one, women would enter the door at the end of the hall, but none of them ever returned. Finally, around 2:00 p.m. I stood to leave, just when my name was called over an intercom.

How different my life would have been had I just kept walking. Against my better judgment, I walked down the hall and through the door to what looked more like an interrogation room than a doctor's office. A man carrying a file entered the room and sat down at the table before me, flipping through its contents without acknowledging my presence in the odd-looking room we now shared.

"Where is Dr. Reimquest?" I asked as politely as I could, but I was seething.

The man continued to scan through his papers while completely ignoring my question and, quite possibly, my very existence.

"This is not the normal office... or his staff..." I said accusingly. The man motioned for me to take a seat with his free hand, while still avoiding me with his gaze. I accepted the seat, the cold metal chair screeching against the floor, echoing my mood. The man kept flipping through until I finally placed my hand over his, stopping his page-turning. Our eyes finally met.

"You're being extremely rude. When someone is speaking to you, you look them in the eye. Don't you have any manners," I hissed. I was expecting to be thrown out, but at this point I didn't care. Instead, the bastard smiled and nodded.

"You're 100 percent correct, and I apologize, Ms. Small," he said, glancing down at his paperwork before meeting my gaze again.

"Lexie, please. Call me Lexie," I said, removing my hand from his.

"Well, Lexie, this office no longer belongs to Dr. Reimquest. Nor the office downstairs, nor the office next to that one. In fact, this entire building is empty of tenants. A very famous plastic surgeon, Dr. Heindle or something, is even no longer a tenant of this building... because what we are doing here is very important and, like most important things, they must also be kept secret." He stared at me, his face blank. I stared back, trying not to show my uneasiness.

"That was a very winded way to say you evicted everyone," I said, then stood up and headed for the door.

"How bad do you want to be a mother, Ms. Small?" The way he asked sounded like he was annoyed he had to ask.

"More than anything," I said, hitting him with a matching tone of annoyance.

He motioned for me to sit, and I hesitantly obliged. He removed his glasses and set them down, then folded his hands, resting his chin on them.

"I'm tired. That's not your fault and I'm sorry... but we have interviewed over 678 women in the past month and, so far, none of you are the right fit." He threw his hands up in a frustrated stretch and leaned back into his chair.

"The right fit for whom?" I asked, concealing my astonishment at the hundreds of candidates before me. "Some celebrity giving up a baby or something?" I asked, and he smiled at this, rocking his chair back and forth with his hands still clasped behind his head.

"No, nothing like that." He stopped moving and placed his hands on the papers across his desk, glancing at them and then up at me as he spoke. "As far as we can tell, it's about two years old. It was found wandering in a field near some hick-town in Nebraska. It was filthy, hungry and, from the look of it, disoriented."

"You found a two-year-old child wandering in a field?" I brought my hand to my lips, covering them as I gasped at the idea of it.

"The couple who found him picked him up and took him back to their farm, where they washed him up and tried to entertain him. They fed him some apple slices and milk and he seemed fine. Eventually, the Doctor showed up to check over the boy. Apparently, some still do house calls. According to the Doctor, the boy appeared healthy enough; strong heartbeat, no broken bones, a little malnourished maybe, so he decided to draw some blood for some tests. It didn't go well." He rummaged through his briefcase and shuffled some pages, spreading them out on the table before me. It looked like a bomb had taken out a kitchen. Broken cups and plates, as well as lumber and porcelain from the sink, littered the ground along with what I could only assume had been three people at one point. A bloody arm still in a white sleeve was surrounded by evidence markers. Another photo showed a charred and still-smoking chest cavity with half-cooked organs clinging to a broken rib cage.

"Is the child okay? Who did this?"

He studied my face for a while, making sure I had seen the carnage clearly and not missed something.

"You are the first person to ask that." He looked astonished, and slightly relieved, as he picked up the phone on the desk.

"We have found the mother. Please send the rest home," and with that one click of a phone call ending, I became a parent.

SSS

"I need to take her vitals," a physician says, peeking over the barrier framing our little box.

David grabs my hand with genuine concern in his wrinkled face.

"Are you in pain?"

"Since I met you." I smiled, gripping his hand.

"She's fine," he said, not taking his eyes off mine.

"That's not how it works," the Doctor replied, still peering down into our box.

David snapped his fingers and noises erupted from the room around them; muffled protests and sneakers squeaking on the floor, and then a door slamming.

"Lex, he's going to get hurt and I can't protect him much longer."

My laugh interrupted him, then grew into a vicious cough and he fed me some water until it subsided. "How did you say that with a straight face?" I asked.

"We have learned things since then, Lex. Came up with new technology based specifically around his physiology."

I was shaking my head before he even finished. "You would have used it already. You would never have let him show you all up like he already has."

"If you think that we haven't been coming up with ways to put him down since the day we found him, you're not as smart as I gave you credit for," he said, now all-business and no pleasure.

"And how did that work out the first time?" I asked, scooting myself up on my pillow. They had set Christopher and I up in a nice one-story house; white picket fence with a backyard, and they even threw in a minivan. They had given Christopher a puppy since statistics showed it helped with anxiety, as well as empathy. After the third 'Baxter' had his skin literally pet *off* of his bones, I told David no more replacements as it would only confuse Christopher. I took Christopher outside and showed him Baxter's mangled body. He looked confused. I grabbed a mouse I had bought at the pet store on my way home from our check-in with David and showed Christopher how to stroke it gently and with little pressure. I held the mouse close and kissed it softly. Then I stroked Christopher's arm to show him the weight and speed I was stroking the mouse. I put it down and it scurried off and into the bushes. Next, I picked up a snail and showed Christopher that I was petting its shell with the same care, and then pushed hard against Christopher's skin as I crushed the snail in my hand.

I wiped the snail on the grass next to Baxter and pointed. Christopher nodded and stroked my arm as slow and as soft as I think he was able to. It felt like sandpaper, but I gritted through it. When he drew blood, he bent back in horror and then grabbed my hand, breaking it. I screamed and fell to my knees as he pulled back again, looking around for help. He came closer and I held my hand up to him, signaling for him to stop. He stood there with his beautiful, blue eyes streaming tears down his face, his hands digging into his palms like deadly weapons finally sheathed. I crawled over to him and held him, telling him everything would be okay. I took his arms and placed them around me, wrapping us in a hug. His weeping into my chest left bruises for weeks. After that, they gave me a glove that had the same amount of force as a crocodile bite. It was meant to punish Christopher. I used it to squeeze his hand when I wanted him to know I loved him.

"The vice-glove had promise. You just used it wrong." David said, shaking his head.

"It worked pretty well when you tried to take him from me." I said, smiling.

One night, while we were sleeping, eight men 'broke into our house.' I heard Christopher screaming and ran to his room. The bullets were occupying Christopher, the ricochets destroying his room and hitting five of the men. His scream alone knocked two others down and one retreated down the hall towards me, grabbing my leg and causing me to fall just short of my nightstand. I kicked furiously, his black-camouflaged body and helmet thudding against my bare foot. I continued kicking, until I saw two red, glowing orbs floating towards us. I froze. The man's curiosity got the better of him, and he turned to see what had spooked me. He fired immediately, sparks illuminating Christopher's face, his eyes glowing like the pits of hell itself. My gloved hand closed around the back of the man's neck, bursting his windpipe like a crimson water balloon, and snapping his head clean off, like a grotesque ice cream cone of viscera.

"We knew it was you, David," I said, staring into his old eyes.

"Of course it was me. Do you have any idea how dangerous it is unless it's controlled?"

"So, we are back to calling him '*It*' now, are we? Jesus Christ, David," I look away from him, disgusted.

He stands and points a finger in front of my face.

"Goddamnit Lex, he is not your KID. We don't even know if he's fucking HUMAN. We know nothing about him. Over 26 years, some of the brightest minds in the world were all paid to study him, and we still know absolute shit! He's hurting people, Lex. He's *killing* people! We should have stopped this when he killed that girl back in high school."

I turned to him abruptly. "That was an accident," I said, anger coating my words.

I remember driving home from the store. The street was caution-taped off, with my neighbors forced to stay in their homes, the windows covered with wooden boards. Soldiers stood in front of each door. My car was halted by four men in hazmat suits pointing their rifles at me. Three loud, rapid taps on the glass and I rolled my window down. I was shouting over the soldier telling me to get out of the car when David came up behind him, pushed him away and pulled open my door.

"David, is he okay? What happened?" I asked, trying to look for Christopher over the cars and shoulders of the men assembled.

"There's been an incident. Christopher is fine but there was a girl…" he wipes his forehead and removes his glasses, obviously frustrated.

"A girl? What are you talking about? Is she okay? CHRISTOPHER!" I yelled as loud as I could, but David's hand clapped over my mouth, hard and tight. I'm trying to scream through it when I heard his voice.

"Mom?... MOM?" Multiple guns rose quickly, pointed at my driveway. I kicked and punched David until I finally broke away and ran into a sea of men, pushing but making no progress.

"MOM!" The word erupted like a sonic boom. Glass shattered, car alarms wailed and everyone covered their ears, which gave me enough room to wiggle through and reach Christopher.

He walked towards me, naked and covered in gore– like someone had thrown a paint-filled balloon of violence at his crotch. I ran and grabbed him as hard as I could, his skin like sandpaper, and his muscles closed around me like a python made of stone, but I didn't care; he was safe, in my arms, and that's all that mattered.

"I didn't…I didn't mean to," Christopher had sobbed. I started to shake as his tears froze and burnt the skin on my shoulder.

"It's alright baby, I know. Everything is okay." David grabbed me and motioned to a car for us to leave, and soon we had arrived at a fully furnished home exactly like our last one, but three states away. We never spoke of it again. Until now.

"He *killed* that girl, Lex. She was only 16 years old. Kristine Prais was her name."

"It. Was. An. Accident," I say, staring into him like an X Ray machine.

"Her skull was shattered and we found her face and brains miles away for Christ sake we had to get her boss at the pizza delivery place she worked at to identify her, Lex," David says defeated.

"They were kids messing around, goddamnit. He didn't know what would happen! How could he know the speed and force that his… Jesus Christ. David, he's allowed to make mistakes."

"Mistakes?" David looks at me like I just slapped him. "You call blowing a girls' head off with your ejaculation a mistake? Like a fucking parking ticket?"

"His first sexual encounter, David. Not only was it embarrassing, but he killed the first person he probably felt he loved! That girl and David would always flirt for gods sake, he had me order pizza 3 times a week just to smile at her and when he finally breaks out of his shell and connects with someone… but what did you do? Did you hug him? Tell him it will all be okay, that it wasn't his fault? No, you brought the fucking army to our door with guns." I nearly spit the words at him.

We sat in silence, neither one of us looking at each other for a while.

"Who do you think has kept him from being locked in a box and thrown into space? Who do you think stopped all those scared-shitless soldiers from blasting him with a million rounds? Who do you think paid off that poor girls parents and gave her a very expensive burial? I'm not his father, Lex, but I did my best to care for him as best I could, too." He crosses his arms and sits back in a pout. Soon, he drops the invisible armor and talks to me like that one night we had together after we arrived in the new town, scared, tired and not knowing what to do next.

"Why is he doing this, Lex? This is what they have always been afraid of; but, until yesterday, he had never proven them right. Why now?"

"You wanted me to raise him so he could be controlled. You wanted a weapon. You followed what you thought were basic ingredients for a perfect, All-American-Boy. Do you remember the first 'husband' you assigned me?"

"George River. He had everything we were looking for: smart, athletic, Christian values; the perfect role model," he said, nodding.

"Abusive."

He shook his head in protest.

"Can you imagine being the man you described and not being able to discipline a child? To be emasculated by a two-year-old boy? For the brightest minds in the world, you people sure don't understand men," I said, cracking a smile. "The first time George hit me, I did my best to hide it. That bruise around my eye. The second time, he busted my lip and Christopher saw it. He was 10 by then. George 'taught him to fly' by throwing him down the stairs. Well, one day I came home and George was at the bottom of the stairs, his jaw severely dislocated. Christopher was eating cereal in the kitchen and watching cartoons. I told him to stay out of the living room until you arrived and took the body away."

"You told me he fell," David said, shaking his head.

"Maybe he did. I don't know, but I know Christopher didn't cry. Not once. The other attempts at giving him a male role model never worked and those men all went back into whatever other secret job you had for them. And it was just me and Christopher. He told me I was sick before we knew it. He cried so loud I had to wear earplugs. Your doctors told me stage four; it was in my bones and I was okay with it, but Christopher wasn't. My son can lift mountains. He can crush a piece of coal in his hands and give me this diamond necklace, but he is powerless against my own cells eating me from the inside out. And that makes him angry. He is angry at what the world is doing. At what people like you have allowed, David. The chemicals in our food. The corruption running our nations and the crime that rules our streets. He's decided he's going to do something about it and there is nothing you can do to stop him." I smiled and sat back, my muscles giving up on me, and surrendered to the drugs.

The sounds around me are foggy now, but I can hear my boy coming to see me. The gunfire sounds like popcorn in a microwave a room away. The grunts and screams resemble a group of terrified children on a carnival ride whooshing past. David is staring at me, pleading with his eyes for me to stop him. I mouth one last question, one that I've always wondered since the day we met.

"The other women, David…What happened to them… The mothers." I hope he heard me. I don't know if I actually got the words out, but his expression divulges the answer. Shame paints his face as his skin starts to turn a faint red, like a lightbulb covered in blood, until two small holes burst forward from his forehead– like worms digging their way through David's brain. David collapses in my lap, his blood splashing my chest and my necklace, the last physical sensation of warmth tucking me in for the end. My beautiful boy stands before me; his red, fire-like eyes cooling rapidly into the bright-blue pearls of hope he has had since the day we met.

"I love you, Christopher. Save them, even if they don't want to be saved."

I close my eyes and hope I did right by him.

Epilogue

Christopher throws the hardcover book across the room, sending it crashing through the wall and leaving an almost cartoonish outline in its wake.

"Goddamnit, Christopher!" His mom yells from the kitchen as he hops up onto the couch, thinking that, somehow, this will prove his innocence. His mother stares at him, hands on her hips. He is defeated and he has been found out.

"I'm sorry, mom," the boy says as he lowers his head, exhaling a little too hard, making the coffee table rattle. His mother rushes over, stopping his glass of Coke from spilling onto the carpet.

"Through your nose, remember? Like we practiced. It slows the airflow."

The boy nods but doesn't match his mother's smile. She sits next to him and brushes the hair from his face, grasping it with two fingers and avoiding the surface of his sandpaper-skin after years of trial and error.

"What's wrong, bud?" She asks, trying not to sound annoyed at his outburst and the new hole in the wall.

"I don't know why I have to read this stupid book every day. Uncle David says I have to and that it's good for me. And you tell me they are good stories to live by."

His mother smirks and tilts her head in a mock shock expression. "How terrible," she says, clutching invisible pearls and finally getting a smile out of the boy.

"No, what I mean is... why is God so mean?" The boy's smile fades, and he breaks his mother's gaze, staring down, fearing what consequence his statement will inspire. To his surprise, his mother is not angry, but nods.

"What do you mean, baby?"

The boy pauses, choosing his words carefully, treading this unfamiliar territory. "I mean, God loves everyone and he's, like, super powerful, but he kills all these innocent kids in Egypt. Like, why didn't he just kill Pharaoh?"

His mother nods and looks around the room as though to see if anyone is listening.

"Is that what you would have done?"

The boy looks at his mother and thinks for a long while.

"I think so," he says, nodding, confidence building with time passing.

"And what about the next one?" his mother asks while picking up the biggest chunks of the wall from the ground.

"The next what?" the boy asks, confused.

"The next Pharaoh. Do you kill him? What about the one after him? Or... do you make yourself Pharaoh?" She says, raising her hands in the air. "When does it stop? When do you stop?"

The boy lay back on the cushion, thinking, then says, "When everyone is safe and free."

His mother continues picking up the debris but pauses to chuckle.

"People don't want to be free. They like being told what to do. They need a King or an Emperor or a God to tell them what to do. The sad fact, Christopher, is that God may have all the power, but he doesn't walk the earth– for whatever reason;

and because he doesn't, he can't be everywhere and can't save everyone. So it is best to do the best you can with the options you have. Nobody can save everyone," she says, her voice sounding defeated but with an acceptance of the fact.

The wind swirls around her and the boy stands before her, holding all of the debris as the wind settles.

"God can." The boy says it as a declaration, displaying absolute faith and confidence. The boy's mother looks at her son, the sun shining in through the space behind him partially blinding her.

"I think you're right," she says, slowly touching his cheek and holding him close until she finally whispers, "And I think we might finally have one who can."

Mind Yours

The man walked into the diner, resembling roadkill. His hair was matted to his forehead with dried blood and chunks of…something. His leather jacket had three long gashes across the back, like an animal, or even a dinosaur by the sheer size of them, had taken a swing at him. The greenish liquid that covered his tattered jeans resembled a bucket of regurgitated glowsticks having been tossed all over them. His shoes were leaving footprints of what looked like a mixture of fresh shit and sand.

Larry watched the man sit in the last booth, facing the wall and resting the large, black garbage-bag he carried between him and the wall. Larry was used to weirdos, *this* job on *this* highway was *loaded* with them and they all needed a place to eat, shit, or just waste his fucking time, like he was sure this bum would. Larry walked out from behind the counter and inhaled, annoyed and instantly regretting his inhale as the man's scent assaulted his nostrils. The man was in way worse shape than Larry had originally thought. His right eye was swollen shut and his nose, although set back into place, had clearly been broken recently and was starting to swell.

"Jesus, buddy! Who took the candy out of you?" Larry exclaimed, eyeing the vagrant who stared straight-ahead at the wall with his one good eye, stroking the bag next to him like a it was a loyal pet.

"I'll have a cup of coffee, please," the man requested, sounding like a nervous actor reading new lines. His volume and pitch were all over the place, correcting himself as he realized it was either too high or too low for its intended audience.

"Buddy, you look like you need a fucking doctor, not a cup of joe," Larry said, putting his hands on his hips and cocking his head, trying to comprehend what had just walked into his establishment. The man didn't say anything to that, just kept stroking the garbage bag until Jerry spun around, grabbed the pot of coffee from the burner and returned to pour until the man's mug was full of liquid energy. Larry gave up on conversation and wasn't going to pay any more attention to this lone customer until, out of the corner of his eye, he could swear he saw the bag twitch.

"Wasn't my fault," the man said, pushing down on the bag roughly and sipping his cup.

"What wasn't your fault?" Larry asked the man, not taking his eyes off of the bag, staring like a hushed paramedic waiting for a patient's chest to rise with life-affirming air.

"My fiancé and I were driving back home from Vegas. We wanted to visit the murder site of that YouTube video but there were so many damn people everywhere it kind of lost its appeal to us."

Larry nodded, still eyeing the seemingly lifeless bag.

"She was always the true crime junkie, not me. I was more into fiction, fantasy, stuff like 'The Lord of the Rings' or 'The Wheel of Time.' Real people... they always kind of creeped me out, ya know what I mean?" The man turned to look at Larry, who finally broke his gaze from the bag and met the man's one good eye.

"Yeah, I definitely know what you mean," Larry said, topping off the man's coffee.

"We hadn't seen anyone for miles and then... He was just walking. Had no water, no food, just him and this garbage bag. I didn't think much of it until Tina said something about him being so damned sunburnt. I drove past him but I looked in the rearview mirror, pulled myself closer to really zoom in on his face. I swear, I almost crushed the brakes. 'That's fucking Josh!' I said to her and then I was pulling the car over. Tina looked at me and the look on her face clearly said "What the fuck are you doing?" and before she could ask, I said, 'I know that guy, we used to go to school together.' So then Josh was walking faster, with his savior– us – from the sun parked just 10 feet in front of him. And she says, 'We are not giving him a fucking ride,' and she locks the doors. I waved her off and unlocked them, saying, "Tina, he'll die in this heat. He was my friend,' I was reassuring her, although, I wouldn't exactly call our *knowing each other* a friendship. The back door opened and the trash bag flew against the other side of the car, thudding against the door and instantly filling the car with a dirty-dog smell, mixed with stale corn chips. Josh quickly followed, placing his left hand on the bag and pulling his door shut. And then he says, 'thanks, we can go now,' like he was entering an uber. I laughed and stared at him for a moment, but all he did was stare back, looking annoyed. And so I said, 'Josh? 'That you, man? It's me, Nate, from school?' But Josh's expression didn't change. All he said was, 'don't know a Nate,' and I could feel Tina's stare burrowing into me; her anxiety level was almost as high as her anger toward me. And she starts to apologize but Josh interrupts, saying 'wait, Nate, from school, yea, I remember now,' and so I nodded like the matter was solved but Tina turned her head toward me as if to say she would never forgive me for this."

Larry set the coffee pot down now, and sat on the other side of the booth, invested in the story. As he groaned into the seat, the old leather making noises, he could swear he heard a moan coming from the bag, but Nate gripped the bag harder, as if choking the bag like it was a living person.

His eyes shifting between the bag and Nate's cyclops-stare, Larry pressed Nate to continue. "Was it your classmate?" He asked, eyeing the bag suspiciously.

"I think so. I can't be sure, though, because he was covered in grime. We didn't get into details because the bag kept stealing my attention." Nate said, looking at the bag.

Larry nodded, looking the bag over again himself.

"We kept driving and finally I asked him what he was doing walking in the heat, but he didn't seem too keen on answering my questions, especially when I asked him what's in the bag."

Larry looked up at Nate, eager to hear the answer. "What did he say?" He leaned in, worried he would miss the answer somehow if he was too far away. Nate finished his coffee and Larry quickly refilled it, urging him to continue.

"He said it was none of my fucking business."

Larry exhaled with laughter, then shook his head.

"And at this point you can imagine Tina's eyes were drilling holes right into my skull and she grabbed my hand, so I laughed it off and told him we came to look at the murder site and maybe get some pictures, but we didn't have any luck. He didn't say anything and just stroked the bag like it was some fucking cat, so I pressed him again, said 'Josh, man, really… What's in the bag?' and he pulls the bag closer to him as I look in the mirror, catching his gaze; his face is turning from annoyed to angry and he says, 'None of your fucking business.' Tina is scared by then and I'm starting to get creeped out as well."

Larry is on the edge of his seat now and the bag is moving on its own, sucking in and out like a gasping man being choked with a grocery bag over his head.

Nate's hands are shaking, but he continues telling his story, needing to hear it himself. Like saying it out loud will somehow make it go away, make this terrible night and this bag go the fuck away.

"So, finally, I pull the car over. I turn the ignition off and I grab Tina's hand as I look Josh dead in his grime-covered eyes and I tell him. I tell him that if he doesn't tell me what's in the bag that he can get out. He can get out of my car and he can walk his ass and his stupid fucking bag to wherever he wants. And as I'm sitting there, my balls sucked up into my stomach like a turtle hiding in its shell, he punches the back of Tina's seat and he kicks it and even spits and says that it's none of my business, to fuck off. Just as I'm about to kick him out, he pushes the door open and walks away. In the opposite direction." Nate's breath is steadying now as he holds the coffee cup tight in his hands.

Larry's eyes look like they are about to bulge from his sockets when he speaks like his life depends upon it. "He left the fucking bag? He left it in your car?" Larry says this like a priest who has witnessed something blasphemous. Nate nods over and over, bringing the cup to his lips and sipping, trying desperately to calm his nerves.

Larry, unable to contain himself, grabs Nate's wrist and begs him with a scream, "What was in the bag?"

Nate suddenly lifts, then smashes the coffee cup down, spilling its lukewarm contents. Soon it is spreading across the table, to the edges, just as Nate shoves the jagged porcelain handle into Larry's jugular. His blood mixes with the murky water and pools around his gasping head until the tiny waves on the surface stop forming from his shallow breaths. Nate stood and looked at the bag, the blood and coffee covering its outer shell and adding to the layers of grime like a tree with new sap hardening over the old. His one good eye finally shifted to Larry as he breathed easy for the first time since he saw that goddamn bag.

As he walked out into the night he finally answered Larry's final question. "That's none of your fucking business."

Don't Take Down Your Fence

    We start with the testicles. We all agreed we wouldn't start there, but we end up going for the most vulnerable of vulnerabilities right away. It screams. At least, it *tries* to scream through the gag fashioned out of two small dresses stitched together. The craftsmanship is amazing. Laura showed us over our last meeting at Starbucks. She had held them flat against her chest displaying the Siamese-twin style dress she had crafted together with a simple Cross Stitch. We were all so impressed that for the next week she'll be teaching a class at the local Youth Center.

    I regret lying to her, but I will not be able to make them myself as I have promised. Jason's soccer practice schedule won't allow me to learn a new craft, even if it *is* as simple as she assures me.

    Margot goes for the nipples next; she pierces them with broken pieces of a toy firetruck. The broken, red plastic darkens to crimson as blood and stretched skin make a Japanese monster-movie scene right before us. If only we had some toy soldiers; we could recreate the scene from The Blob– a rubbery jelly mold swallowing cars and people in its wake. Only our blob would be made of stretched skin and a pierced, hairy nipple.

    Margot sticks her tongue to one side of her mouth, not satisfied with just the truck. She starts in on the next side of his chest, adding the green, broken army-helicopter from her pocket. Pretty soon, if she happens to have a toy police car, we'll have a fully established emergency service inside of him. So far, it's going well.

Nobody has passed out from the blood, nobody has had to step outside to vomit, nobody (out of necessity and not pleasure) has eaten the fresh-baked chocolate-walnut cookies Christopher made that Margot always wins the church auction with. Last year, she took home three dozen for $50, not a steep price once you taste them, I promise. But I was saving for Maddy's cheer conference at the time and my sweet tooth had to suffer for it. Rebecca is doing what she does best, disposing of the paper plates and half-empty cups of her famous pink lemonade. She hands me a cookie and offers me fresh gloves. I take both and hand her my bloody pair. I smile and she grins back, stuffing the soiled contents into the industrial trash cans Richard bought with cash, a town over.

Richard can be a bit of an annoyance, but he means well. His paranoia shows through as he triple-gloves his hands. The latex is so tight on his fingers that he can't grip the power drill sitting next to the fresh-squeezed juice from his own orchard. He drops it after playing with it for a moment and we all snicker, like kids in a library.

"Yeah, laugh it up, but you won't be laughing when they sweep the place for fingerprints," he says, smugly.

We all get back to work as I pull up the anatomy of a human on my phone while the others keep focused on the table. I pull the makeshift gag out of its mouth, but I can't see the parts of his tongue I'm going to burn clearly. It starts to moan and everyone in the room pauses. We all look at each other, smiling and nodding as a sense of accomplishment washes over us. We should be proud; none of us have done anything like this before. Hell, half of us have never even killed an *animal* before.

The sheriff had asked us all, as we stood in a line with flashlights in hand, if anyone had hunted these words before? It was a good question, but you could tell by looking at us the answer was a chorus of No. Most of us didn't even remember to wear hiking boots, and the rest didn't even own a pair. Some of us weren't too worried because Megan was a playful child and she had wandered off before. Usually, she was found as far as a puppy or butterfly could travel before stumbling upon one of our yards. We would bring her in and wait for Richard to come get her.

It had been two days when Richard's panic began to spread amongst all of us. We searched. We searched in idiotic places, under large rocks and tangled bushes that no child could even fit in. It was a frantic hope. No, it was a serious desperation.

Margot lifted all of our spirits on the ninth day. "They've brought dogs!" She yelled with a smile. Big Bloodhounds and German shepherds could cover more forest floor than any of us could. The dogs all started barking and rushed towards the Creek. Deputies were rewarding the dogs when they stopped us from approaching, all except Richard. They escorted him down to the Creek.

An hour later he came back, stumbling past us. He had been crying. His eyes looked like they had been drinking at a frat party. What we all noticed the most was that he was walking alone.

"Rich?" We dared to ask as he walked right past us, his face void of emotion. He stopped, but didn't turn to answer us.

"They aren't search and rescue dogs," he said, then kept walking. We all dropped our gazes, trying to mentally crawl into, and hide inside, our own skin.

"I don't understand," Margot had said, her hope fading into panic.

I started in the direction of my home, looking back over my shoulder to ease Margo's confusion. "Cadaver dogs," I muttered, then continued walking away.

We all covered for Rich. I opened his shop on days he didn't show up or answer his phone. Nobody dared to bother him at his house. The funeral came and went, and Rich seemed worse each day.

"Megan had drowned." The Sheriff said simply, but with a hint of disbelief. Margot, as usual, howled. However, we were all curious because there was slight bruising on Megan's neck and the back of her head. We didn't think too much of it at the time though, the sheriff assured us the bruises most likely came from her tumbling down into the Creek. None of us could imagine the pain Rich was suffering through.

That night when Margot got off work, she picked up Brian, her six-year-old son, and promptly spoiled him rotten. She bought him every sweet and salty thing his heart desired, and he finally got the brand-new diecast fire truck he had been asking for every time they passed its display in the mall.

Things went back to normal and soon the usual routines set in again. Rich finally came out of his shell and attended church more and more. It was good to have Rich back, but we could all tell he wasn't whole. He would watch Brian play with his toys and sadness would swell in his eyes. Looking back, Rich should have been the constant reminder to us that we weren't untouchable. As the thought crosses my mind, I begin carving. The surgical steel box-cutter I ordered on Amazon is definitely getting a five-star rating. The blade glides through the pink, thin flesh of its eyelids like they're butter. I can tell It's staring at me. It has no real choice at this point. I curse myself as blood pools in the eye socket. I hadn't counted on that. I grab the Fiji water from the table and take a swig, then rinse the eye until the crimson canvas becomes a pinkish white. The thing looks like it has a terrible case of pink eye and I am reminded of the time when nearly the whole school had come down with a "poop-eye-demic," as Margot had put it. Her son, Brian, and my daughter, Maddie, had spared the poop-eye fiasco. It was nothing serious— check each child for symptoms, wash the pillows, all the usual stuff. I was beginning to gather my coat when Maddie returned to the gym. "You all set, baby girl?" I had asked, but before she could answer, someone was screaming. It was Margot, and she was searching the crowd desperately, calling out to Brian. I tried to calm her down, but she wasn't having it. She grabbed Maddie by the shoulders and asked her what happened, where was Brian, she was supposed to be playing with Brian. Maddie was crying because she didn't know what she had done wrong to make Brian's mom so scary.

"Brian was happy to go," she said. The man in the truck had shown Brian and her an army helicopter that would go well with Brian's fire truck. They had just left to go get one that Brian could keep, and they would be right back.

Margot began to mentally shatter before us. She froze. It was like seeing an ocean freeze mid-tidal wave. She calmly turned and then lowered herself onto the cold, metal chair. She began to shake her head side to side as the rest of us ran outside, looking for what we knew was already gone.

I grilled Maddie with question after question. "What did the truck look like? What did the man look like?" She was crying through every answer, knowing something was wrong and feeling blamed for it, without knowing what she was blamed for. We all did our duty; again, we searched. We didn't sleep, we printed and dispersed flyers. The dogs found the fire truck and the green helicopter shattered on a rock near an old cabin. The blood found inside the cabin was tested and the results confirmed our worst fears: it was Brian's.

 Margot would sit outside on her porch, every day, with the shattered toy's parts resting in her lap. Sometimes, when the rain was bad, one of us would go and cover her, but she never left the porch except to eat and use the restroom. Maddie asked me what she was doing out there all the time, and I told her the only thing that made sense; she's waiting for Brian to come home.

 Months passed.

 Richard had formed a neighborhood watch. He even made a jacket for Mark. It made us feel safe. Well, at least, safer.

 Things were starting to calm down when suddenly Laura stopped showing up at church and one day we stopped by to check on her. A Sheriff answered and told me to come inside, but to leave Maddie in the car. I walked inside and found Laura on the couch, a blanket draped over her. She was bruised and her swollen, left eye looked like a squeezed lemon producing tears.

 "I found her upstairs," John, the sheriff, stated. "She was tied to the bed, and she's been, well…" I nodded, silencing him.

 I approached Laura and she shivered away in defense. "Laura, honey, it's me. Where are Emma and Abby?" She just stared, her lips beginning to quiver. "Where are the twins?" I asked again, looking at the sheriff. Surely, he had checked on them.

 "They're missing," he said, lowering his eyes to the floor. The world seemed to fade away in a cacophony of sounds. Laura knew that her children were lost to her. Laura would later explain to us in grief counseling, formerly the book-club, that she had woken up around 3:00 a.m. to check on the girls. Matt was out of town for business, and she hated sleeping alone. So sometimes she would let the girls sleep with her. All she remembered was opening the girl's door and seeing their beds empty and ransacked. Then her head erupted in pain and she saw black. She woke up naked and tied to the bed. Two days passed before the sheriff found her. She had been dehydrated, starving and was out of tears.

Hours later, the lynch mob was in full swing. The whole town showed up, demanding blood. Sheriff John was answering questions the best he could, but we were angry and, even worse, we were scared. John explained that he needed help from all of us, that we needed to be on the lookout for the missing girls. We told him to start looking for the guy in the truck that took Brian. It had to be the same man responsible.

John's response was not what we expected. "There is no evidence these crimes are connected." We all roared with curses and tiffs.

"We've got a fucking serial killer loose and you ain't doing a fucking thing," Christopher yelled, while holding his newborn son tight. Jack sighed heavily as he shifted through the cards on the podium, then looked out at the fuming crowd. He looked as if he knew this was coming, but no matter how hard he tried, he was not prepared for it. "We as a Community, and especially as a law enforcement agency, can't treat this as a serial killer. In a case where a serial killing is established, three victims must be linked in murder."

None of us spoke. We looked to Sheriff John as our scapegoat; we needed someone to blame for our fear. And Sheriff John... poor John had just lit the fire for us. Things were thrown, paper cups, chairs, shoes. All manner of objects were hurled towards John as fast as the angry shouts were.

"You piece of shit!"

"You mean we gotta wait for more of our kids to die?"

John retreated into the station, defeated. The meeting room slowly emptied and, eventually, only a few of us were left; we looked like a family waiting in a hospital while a loved one was being saved or fading away. I looked around the room. Margot was holding Brian's toys clenched to her chest, staring off into space. Richard looked out the window, his head resting against his arm. Laura was cleaning up the trash thrown at John just to keep busy. Christopher rocked his baby boy to sleep.

I broke the silence. "We can't wait anymore."

They all looked up at me.

"The cops ain't doing a damned thing and I… I can't let anything happen to my kids. Or anyone else's. We need…" I started to tear up and I had their attention. "We need to kill him, whoever this is. We need to hunt him down and kill him."

They all continued to stare at me, not a single one of them blinking.

"Yeah, if only Bud," Richard finally said, looking back to the window and sighing.

"I'm serious," I said, standing up and addressing them all. "We'll set a trap. We'll catch him and we'll kill him, just like any other pest."

"I'm in," Christopher chimed in, quietly, looking at his baby boy.

Richard turned back to face us, incredulous, and said. "You're really serious about this?" Christopher and I looked at each other, then back to Richard, and nodded. Richard rubbed the back of his neck and sat down next to Laura. She put her hand over Richard's. "I'm in, too," she said, then nodded to us. Richard held Laura's hand and nodded to us as well, tears wetting his big cheeks.

"Okay. We find him and we kill him. For our kids," Richard said. We all nodded to one another; our cause was established.

"No." It was the first time Margot had spoken since Brian had gone missing. We started to question her when Margot stood and walked towards us. A rage was heavy in each one of her tiny footsteps. Her hands shook with anger. She got close. Uncomfortably close.

"We don't kill him. We destroy him," she said, tears leaving her focused, unblinking eyes. We all looked down and then around to each other. We all nodded one last time. We were going hunting.

The thing on the table keeps staring at me, its one unbloodied eye focused solely on me and the terror I'm submitting it to. I should feel bad. Any normal person would. But, I don't. They can't either for this to work. Everything is going according to plan and pretty soon they will all be able to put this behind them.

After we had established our cause, we met at Starbucks the next day to discuss the plan.

Margot was becoming herself again. She was talking about all of the horror movies she had binge-watched the night before, and the medieval torture methods she had googled throughout the day. We all slurped our Frappuccinos and shared body-disposal methods while passing around a plate of chocolate croissant samples the barista had recommended.

Who would set the bait at the upcoming fair? Tons of people would be around and it would be unlikely anyone would notice a child go missing. The perfect bait for our killer was a child. I volunteered to use my son, Jason, as our bait. The others thanked me and praised my bravery. I would leave Jason 'unattended' by the animal stocks. The sheep and cows were a free exhibit, but almost nobody ever went there for more than a couple of minutes. If a child was to be abducted, we all agreed that's where it would happen.

I tried my best to not be nervous, but as a parent you never want harm to come to any of your children. I was absolutely certain Jason would be unharmed, but the father in me was still nervous and scared. I had left Jason at the petting station and informed him I would be back soon. I kissed him and hugged him tight, then walked away and moved into position next to Richard. Laura was waiting with the van she used to haul the twins to ballet practice; it was oversized and perfect for what we needed.

Margot and Steven were waiting at the hotel room that was done up for our night of revenge. The hotel was under renovations but, luckily, Richard was a majority shareholder in the company. He could come and go as he pleased; we would have the whole place to ourselves until 8:00 a.m. the next morning.

We waited for what seemed like an eternity, and Jason was getting bored and anxious. Finally, seemingly from nowhere, a man appeared and, to our delight, he was approaching Jason. "Hi, are you Jason?" The man asked, moving right up to our bait. Jason nodded, clearly nervous. The man reached into his coat and produced a Snickers bar as he said, "Your dad sent me to get you. He told me these were your favorite." Jason took the candy and carefully examined it. Jason was diabetic and he knew he wasn't allowed *any* candy. Nobody in their right mind would think *I* would tell a stranger to give my diabetic son candy. I was hopeful Jason would think the same but, to my distress, he opened the candy, tore off a generous bite and began to chew. I pounced; Richard was right beside me. He tackled the man as I slipped the gag over his mouth. He was yelling and kicking, cursing us the entire time. Jason was confused, but he did as I said and ran home to his sisters.

Once the man was in the van, it was easy. Richard continued punching him, and I didn't stop him from spending the 15-minute drive using it as a punching bag.

Once we began moving it from the van to the table, he started to come to. "What… What the fuck, man? You. You?"

I shut him up quickly with a blow to the nose. He was ready for *our* justice system now. The night went on and we took turns on him; cutting, scraping, burning. Hours later, the moment was upon us. The surgical masks concealing our identities were just itching to come off, to show this bastard who had destroyed him.

"Where are they?" Laura roared while Margot twisted the broken pieces of toy into the perverted thing's nipples to emphasize the query. It screamed and writhed in pain.

"He can't answer you," I said, holding up its tongue for them to see. I shoved a pen into its still-functioning hand and asked, "Where did you take the children?"

It's one good, bloodshot eye stared at me while It wrote, and when he finished, I snatched the paper up and crumpled it in my hand.

"What did it say?" The question echoed around the room, like an empty parking ramp, leaving one person's lips and emerging from someone else's.

"Fuck you," I said, laughing it off. I started to punch that lonely good eye and before long, the others joined in. We all screamed, over and over, "Fuck you, too," each punch and kick a physical reply to his last scribbles of defiance. We continued cursing and kicking long after It released its final breath. We all met each other's gazes, a sense of pride paired with acceptance washed over us. We had rid the world of something evil, and we were okay with that.

We left at different times, as previously agreed. I volunteered to oversee the disposal of the body. I told the others that I would take the burden because they all deserve some time to reflect on, and hopefully accept, what tragedies had befallen them at the hands of It. Margot hugged me and told me to make sure Brian's toys were destroyed with the body. She was ready to accept the unacceptable.

The next week at church, our little town was back to normal. We shared recipes and swapped movie suggestions for the picnic in the park. Laura moved up in the ranks of community watch. She still hopes to find the twins one day, but has accepted that their bodies might be lost forever.

Richard teaches woodshop now, part-time, at the local high school; he says it keeps his mind busy and reminds him of the birdhouses he used to make with Megan. Christopher baked up a storm and wrapped up a big plate of his famous cookies for each of us. We all knew what we were celebrating and nodded a silent thanks. Most nights, Margot hugs me and thanks me for showing them what needed to be done to help them move on and get over the hatred and fear that the monster had put them through. And most nights, as I walk home and snack on my fresh batch of thank you goodies, I think to myself how easy it was.

Through each candy-coated crunch, I think of Margot thanking me.

Through each chopped pecan I grind through my teeth, I think of the sound Megan made when she realized we wouldn't be leaving the woods together.

As the crumbs fall on the wet asphalt, I think of the rolls of cash I dropped at the drifter's feet to 'kidnap my little boy' from my 'custody-battle-bitch of a wife' and how he smiled as I handed him a shiny new helicopter toy to give my son.

As I struggle with my keys and enter my house, I think of Laura and how good her flaccid body felt under mine. Walking down the steps, I allow myself one last treat. The group's favorite: double peanut butter fudge brownies; I make sure to leave the cookies on the plate. Cleaning off the mess all over myself, I throw the remaining treats into the dog kennel at the bottom of the basement, eliciting soft whimpers and ravenous moans. My chin is covered in Reeses goodness. I pull out the remnants of my pockets and wipe my face with the piece of paper I crumpled up from the poor drifter's last message, the chocolate and peanut butter sludge merging with his broken hope of exposing me. The paper was now a diarrhea-looking mess, but if you were looking close enough, you could make out the poorly written *YOUR HOUSE*.

I laugh and toss the paper towards the debris and collection of confectionary-carnage on the kennel floor. Dusting myself off, I walk back upstairs and lock the soundproof door behind me. Recalling all of this always makes me not want to haul the bowls upstairs to fill them with dog food. It looks like Brian and the twins will have to make do with cookies for dinner again tonight.

Caduceus

Elise felt nervous walking through these woods alone, especially so late in the evening. The fog around her felt oddly appropriate considering her feelings as of late. She didn't know where to go nor what lay ahead; she had walked endlessly, whispering those dreaded words *what if?* She shook her head and focused on the road. Nicholas had told her to stay on the path and to make it fast, so nobody questioned why she was gone from her workstation for so long.

"Can't you accompany me? I don't want to do this alone," she had pleaded to the man. He took her hands in his, as he always did, so she would feel comforted, safe. His hands were soft, not like her brother's or her father's who worked in the fields and the mines. His hands revealed his station and she felt important whenever he touched her with them.

"You will be fine. And when this is over, we will be together. Now, go." And with that she was ushered into the fog, both of the forest and of her own thoughts. She had heard stories, of course. These 'women of the woods,' as they were called, were popular among the girls' scary stories they told each other when the headmistress would call for bed.

Each gnarled tree looked like it was judging her as she walked past. Her new dress, a gift from Nicholas, dragged behind her, collecting leaves and mud like a fancy corpse tied to the back of a wagon.

She focused on her feet, but couldn't help hearing the giggles and snickers of past tales repeat in her mind.

"I heard they eat them," one would whisper.

"I heard they drink the blood," someone would counter.

The monstrosities would grow, along with the volume of the laughter, and eventually the headmistress would storm in. The girls would scatter like mice, all pretending to be asleep as she stalked each aisle like a sheep-dog making sure its flock was all accounted for.

When she had first met Nicholas, it was to deliver campaign banners the girls had been commissioned to sew for him. He looked at her like no other man, other than her uncle, had ever looked at her and the initial feelings of excitement overtook her. They would see each other around town and at church every day. She could feel him staring at the back of her head as she sang praise to the lord. She was always standing in the front with her classmates, and Nicholas was seated in the rafters with his wife and children and the others who ran things far above her worries.

It wasn't long before she was being called in the middle of the night, woken by her headmistress and ushered into a carriage to 'discuss' campaign designs with Nicholas. The first time he kissed her was soft and sweet, the way a mother kisses the head of her child. Soon, Elise felt those kisses were more of a formality when compared to the more ferocious way Nicholas now kissed her lips. Sometimes she imagined a great, sucking octopus and would giggle, which made Nicholas smile and take it as encouragement to kiss her even harder.

Her visits became nightly and when her work suffered for it, nobody ever mentioned it. She felt important, and that felt good. Nicholas's power around town became her own. People stepped aside for her in the bread-lines, new dresses were delivered to the school from various shops, and soon, Nicholas had her moved to an apartment closer to his office. He was becoming more of hers with each day and soon she would be living in the house with him and his children.

Some nights they would argue about her staying in 'her cage' as she now liked to call it, beautiful as it was, but Nicholas would end those with his hands in one way or the other. She was used to the slaps, it was how she had been brought up. But she had never been *hit* before and she did not enjoy it. She much preferred it when Nicholas would end their arguments with his hands between her legs. She enjoyed the cold feeling of his wedding ring warming inside her with each movement of his soft hands, each shudder going through her wetness, the ring like a lightning rod inside her, each movement a broken vow of ecstasy. Afterwards, when he had finished, she would lay close to his chest until he would leave for his daily duties of the town or back to his wife's bed. The night before her journey, as he prepared to leave, she told him she was with child and, though she had not expected happiness, she surely wasn't expecting how cold he became.

"There is a woman who will take care of it." Elise held her still-small belly and shook her head, then said, "I won't have another raise it."

Nicholas paused in the middle of putting on his boots, then laughed when he realized she was serious. He ended the conversation quickly, with no discussion; just a shake of his head and a simple, chuckled word, "No."

Looking at the path ahead, she could have protested more but she had seen what happened to girls who tried to keep such children, and this *was* the only way forward. The vines on the old, metal gate made it almost impossible to see through, but Elise could see the broken-down farmhouse clear enough. With one strong tug, the gate tore through the mud as it made a half circle in front of her, almost like a warning– a friend holding up arms, saying *wait a minute*. She ignored her fear and strode down the stone path toward the ivy-wrapped brick. The sign on the door looked ominous; she couldn't read, it was forbidden of her sex, but the symbol was an image of a stick, a serpent wrapped around it with two wings protruding on either side. She didn't know what it meant but she had been taught her whole life to be afraid of snakes; her fear made her take a step back from the door now.

She froze in place, her body heavy, like a stone had been placed on her head. She dropped to her knees, her pretty dress now a fancy rake, picking up the 'breadcrumbs' and eliminating any trace of her ever coming to this place. No way to find her way home to Nicholas.

"Home," she chuckled, looking back at the open gate stuck in the mud. Her trance was broken by the sound of the old, rotten wood squeaking open. She turned and hurried to wipe her tears, then glanced up to meet the gaze of a woman peeking out of the slit, her wrinkled hand displaying lines of age like rings on the trees the woodsmen cut down.

The door opened more to reveal the old woman and her tiny, hunched over frame. Besides her hair, which was unkempt and gray, her features were not the wrinkled and toothless maw, nor the crooked nose and yellow eyes, her classmates had described in scary stories of witches.

"You alone?" The witch asked, looking through the door and squinting her eyes like the sun was shining bright around them; judging by the witch's pale flesh it might, indeed, be bright to her.

Elise nodded.

"You a mute?"

Elise shook her head.

"Can you walk?"

Elise stood, brushing off her dress as best she could.

The witch nodded and turned away, beckoning Elise in with her hand.

Elise watched her disappear, the darkness of the house swallowing her fragile frame.

"I'm old and could die any minute so if you want something you better get in here," the witch called from somewhere deep inside.

Elise hurried through the door, shutting it softly behind her and letting her eyes trace the walls, where pieces of old paper hung with fancy letters, and portraits of a young woman standing with others. There were jars full of plants and other nondescript, floating things, which Elise dared not try to identify. Tools lay on a silver tray with bowls of water, and bloodied rags cradled some of them like a loaf of bread from the market– or fresh flowers, like the ones Nicholas sometimes brought her.

"Sit." The witch startled her from behind with the order, but she did as she was told and sat in the first open chair by the table.

The Witch sat across from her and sipped tea from her cup.

"How far along are you?' she asked as she sipped.

Elise looked down at her stomach. "I… I'm not sure."

"When was the last time you had your blood?" The Witch was writing things down as she spoke.

"Oh, eight…maybe nine weeks," Elise said after thinking it over.

The Witch stood and shuffled over, placing a listening device on Elise's abdomen and shushing her even though Elise did not speak.

"Remove your clothing and lay on the table."

Elise grabbed her dress and slowly let it drop to the floor, covering her breasts not out of shame but more from the cold of the drafty, old house.

"Will it hurt?" Elise asked as she lay on the table, spreading her legs.

The witch was now boiling water in the kitchen, chuckling as she answered, "Yes, but I have herbs to make you numb if you have the money for them," she said, pouring the water into the bowl and placing a large needle inside.

"He…Nicholas gave me money, it's in my dress," Elise said, patting her knees with her nervous fingers.

The Witch scrubbed her hands and dried them off, echoing the name.

"Nicholas. He's a popular one. Third girl this month," she said, shaking her head.

Elise didn't understand what this meant, and she didn't like her tone.

"You're not as ugly as I was told," Elise said, her own tone sharper than she intended.

"Magic," the old Witch proclaimed, waving her hands before her and smiling warmly.

Elise smiled back, the anger leaving her. "Is it true you made a pact with the devil, and you eat the babes?" She asked the question like a curious child, giddy for the details.

The old witch laughed and held up the needle before her. "I never made a pact, but I did take an oath once. When they first came, a lot of us thought it would all blow over. Then they started to put us on trial, and then…" The witch's smile fades, and she stares down at the floor wiping away a tear and fixing her glasses. "It doesn't matter. I get to live free from *them* and they send me you girls. It's funny. *You* aren't allowed to make the decision, only they are. And when it comes down to it… people like me will always exist solely because they need us to clean up their messes and keep their secrets."

Elise nodded, pretending to understand; just how she was taught ever since she was a child.

"Nicholas says we can be together if we do this. If we take care of it we can live happily together." Elise says hopefully, like saying the words out loud will make it true.

"We," the witch chuckles and then her expression grows serious. "Do you see him anywhere? Is he here next to you holding your hand? There is no 'we,' girl."

Elise sat up and slapped the witch, startling herself as much as the old woman now holding her cheek. Elise covered her mouth in embarrassment and the two women stood in silence, staring at each other until the witch started laughing, paving the way for Elise's own laughter to spill out.

"You don't have to do this if it's not what you want. There are places you can go. There are always options… that's why I still do this. Your body is not a cage with someone else holding the key, dear." The witch grabbed Elise's hand and smiled, squeezing it in short bursts of reassurance.

Elise squeezed back, nodding and looking to the door, but ultimately back at her belly where her future, regardless of her decision, waited in anticipation. The cramps were like a swarm of angry bees more than butterflies, and try as she might to breathe through the nerves, her panic was getting the better of her.

"I can't breathe," Elise gasped in a shy voice, excusing the suffocation like a sneeze or a cough.

"It's alright, dear, drink this. It will calm you, but it's very strong so…" Elise emptied the cup in one gulp, sparing only the drops that fell from her rushed consumption.

"Oh, dear." The witch smirked, covering her mouth with her hand. "Okay, let's lay you down and try to keep calm." She helped Elise lay down, tucking a pillow behind her head. When Elise was settled, the witch put on a long, tattered white coat and gathered up some odd-looking tools.

"Were you born a witch? Was your mother one, I mean," Elise asked, still trying to slow her breathing.

The witch again chuckled to herself, then continued to sterilize her instruments. "My mother was a librarian."

This surprised Elise.

"Did they…" she asked, dreading the answer too much to finish the question.

"Oh yes, the whole building," the witch replied, void of any emotion.

"I'm sorry," Elise said softly, looking at the old witch.

She stopped cleaning her tools and looked into Elise's green eyes, then said, "I believe you," before nodding and slowly easing Elise's legs open.

"Will this hurt?" Elise asked again, looking over her spread legs to the witches bent-down forehead.

"You or the fetus?" the witch asked while pulling medical-grade gloves on.

"The what?" Elise scrunched her brow in confusion. The witch sat back in her chair.

"You want to know if the baby will feel pain?" she asked, sympathetically.

Elise nodded.

"No. From what I can recall, the last study showed that it took 24 weeks before the receptors for pain are formed, and from what you have told me, you are nowhere near that."

Elise still didn't quite understand it all, but she understood enough to find comfort in that thought.

"Do you think he loves me? Truly loves me?" Elise sat up as much as she could to see the answer in the witch's face.

"Psychology was never my field, dear," the witch held open her hands in surrender.

The two stared at each other in a silent agreement of what her response truly meant. The witch hadn't said the word, but Elise was pretty sure the answer boiled down to "no."

"I think he loves you as all men have loved girls like you. In a way, he believes he loves you and probably feels protective of you even, but what you have in your belly there threatens his power, and men will always love power more than any girl."

Elise smiled, then nodded while wiping tears away.

"Will you help me up? Elise asked, extending her arms towards the old witch.

The witch sighed and slipped off her gloves. "You are sure?"

Those three little words were such a simple question and yet, such an impossible thing to answer.

Elise nodded.

As they said their goodbyes and the witch walked her to the door, she was taken aback by the tight grip Elise embraced her in, warmed by the 'thank you' that was whispered through her hair and into her old ears.

The old witch watched the girl as she disappeared down the path, soon swallowed by the fog and the night.

🍄🍄🍄

That evening, Elise slept warm and safe in her bed, brushing off the worries of what tomorrow would bring upon her and her still-alive, unborn child.

She awoke to Nicholas playing with her hair, a single white rose beside her.

She held it to her nose, taking a deep breath, then noticed its stale, plastic aroma.

"Afraid the newest batch haven't been scented yet," Nicholas said, setting the fake flower to the side. "We probably should have kept some growing for special occasions, but you remember– 'A crop we can't eat, is a crop we don't need,'" he said in a mock-serious tone.

Elise smiled, rubbing the sleep from her eyes.

"So how are you feeling?" Nicholas asked, fixing his appearance while looking in the mirror to the side table.

"I'm fine, actually," Elise said.

"Good! See, I told you, nothing to worry about. That witch always does a good job."

"Have you seen her before?" Elise at Nicholas; perhaps she had misheard.

"What do you mean, dear?"

"You said she always does a good job. How many times have you met her?"

Nicholas stopped fixing his tie and turned to grasp Elise's hands. "She helps many men around town with these... situations," he said with a smile.

"If she helps them, why is she forced to live alone in the woods? Beyond the town. She is very kind and *very* smart."

Nicholas gripped her hands tighter as he spoke. "That woman is everything that was wrong with this country. They wanted equality and when we gave them a morsel of it, they destroyed industries overnight with rumors and accusations. Men who built empires crumbled from words and hashtags, and for what? No, that woman, that *witch*, that fucking *baby-killer* is exactly where she belongs... Away from decent people and decent society." Nicholas was breathing heavily now.

"You're hurting me" Elise whispered, trying not to incite another outrage. Nicholas loosened his grip and kissed her on the cheek.

"No matter, our little problem is fixed and now everything can go back to normal." Elise looked down at her belly and then back to Nicholas. He paused, noticing her eyes and what confession they were conveying. Nicholas started rubbing his face and pacing.

"You'll go back today. Now, right now!" He was yelling, his pace quickening.

"I will not," she was shaking her head before the words even left her lips.

Nicholas was upon her now, his hand pushing her face into a squashed-up mess. "You think you're smart now? Is that it? That old bitch tells you how it *used* to be and all of a sudden you think you can do whatever you want, hm?"

Elise was weighing her options. She wouldn't win in a fight because she was too small. She could run, but, where to?

Nicholas pushed her away, disgusted.

As he turned to close the door, he paused and looked into her mask of confusion, pain and sadness.

"I loved you, you know that?"

Elise looked down at her belly and inhaled a deep breath. "I believe you *think* you did," she said, nodding. It wasn't what Nicholas was expecting but it's what he would need to accept, for it was all she had left to give him.

☥ ☥ ☥

The witch woke to the sound of horns blowing. She looked at her watch; it was a half hour before noon. She was old and not as fast as she used to be, but she could make it if she hurried. She knew the shortcuts of the woods and ways to get into the city without being seen. She covered her face with her shawl and began her quickened pace towards the center of the city.

The center of town was bustling with people, as was to be expected whenever an execution was to take place. The states had ruled lethal injection too costly for taxpayers years ago so the new method of hanging with the invention of the "Quick Noose" took hold. The device was made of a wired, steel cable; its inner circle placed around the neck was lined with thin sheets of razor, making for a quick beheading. The old witch drew no attention to herself while making her way slowly to the center of the gathered crowd. She sighed heavily when she saw what she had been fearing since the horns had sounded.

The girl who had visited her the night before was bound in the stocks. Bruises blackened both of her eyes and blood dribbled from her cracked lips. She didn't know if the girl could see her, but she looked at the poor woman's eyes; she would be with her through this as much as she could be.

"Welcome, citizens," a nice-looking man yelled out across the crowd. "Today, we are here to pass judgment on an unfortunate soul who has turned away from God, our laws and our country." Cheers erupted all around the witch. She had seen this barbarism before, but it still made her shake in anger every time she witnessed it.

"This Woman, Elise Matelassé, is guilty of the following…" The good-looking man is handed a clipboard from the soldier whose face is covered, but not with the usual "Great Again" flag mask, just a simple, white cover making him stand out amongst the rest of the carbon-copied tactical soldiers lining the stage.

"The offenses are as follows: One, one count of conspiring to commit infanticide. Two, one count of infanticide. Three, consumption of an unapproved non-Church/Government medicine. Four, being unaccompanied past 9:00 p.m.. The first three charges have been combined into the grandfathered law of Witchcraft and thus, a new charge of treason has been added. The sentence for these crimes is death, which will be carried out thusly."

Elise tried to speak but the white-faced soldier cracked her hard against the mouth, causing her head to slam into the wooden stock. The witch prayed (something she had not done since the death of her mother) that Elise was knocked out and would just sleep through what was to come.

The soldier unraveled the shiny noose like a lasso and placed it over Elise's head. He pulled it taut, the blades quickly trickling blood from around Elise's strained neck. To the witch's disappointment, the sudden, sharp pain woke Elise, and she let out a scream.

"If anyone wishes to defend the honor of this witch you must do so now." Nobody moved; defending anyone against treason usually landed you in the same position. The witch thought for a moment, then started to raise her arm, but felt a tug on her hand, her strength no match for the soldier at her side. They locked eyes and he simply shook his head.

She didn't see it happen; her eyes had been on the soldier restraining her arm when she heard the "pop" of the lasso being pulled tight. The crowd erupted, cheering as Elise's head landed with a wet thud on the stage. The good-looking man kicked at it, launching the head into the bloodthirsty crowd where they spat on it and played games with it, scaring each other by passing it around as the younger boys grabbed it and threw it at their mates.

The witch pushed through the crowd and grabbed the head by its long, dirty hair. She glared at anyone who dared try and take it from her. The crowd's attention quickly turned back to the stage for the next item on the agenda and the old witch took her leave with Elise's head in tow.

The witch cleaned Elise's face in the sink as best she could. It was still swollen and stretched, and she didn't like to look at it. She could feel Elise staring at her, judging her for not doing more.

"You stupid girl," she was whispering, to herself as much as to the head. "You should have left; you should have saved yourself and left!" She collapsed onto the counter, sobbing into the sink, her hair mingling with Elise's and forming a rattail of gray and red.

The old witch remembered the way the girl had held her hand and looked into her eyes for guidance. The sadness began to leave her withered, old frame and rage boiled up from deep in her sagging belly until it oozed from her pores. Hot tears streaked her face, saliva poured out of her mouth like a snake escaping her throat, fearful of the enraged howl following it. The witch was mad and the witch was smart.

The witch worked all night preparing the herbs and peeling the skin and, sure enough, a knock woke her early the next morning.

The witch opened the door expecting some sad, broken thing to greet her. Instead, before her stood a well-dressed man looking around to make sure he had not been followed.

"I am Nicholas Hatten, I bel..."

The witch left the door open, beckoned him inside and walked back into the house to prepare her tea. Nicholas entered and closed the door. He looked at the pictures and Medical degrees from various universities on the walls, noticing a photo of what seemed to be new doctors at a graduation ceremony and the name that read DR. LISA BREANNE

"This you?" Nicholas pointed to the young blonde in the white coat. The witch nodded and poured the tea, handing him a cup. He sniffed it, not appearing overly impressed with the aroma. "I believe my friend Elise paid you a visit to get a procedure done." He wasn't looking at her out of fear, he wasn't afraid per se, but she could tell he was nervous and that was something he wasn't used to. He reminded her of the R.N. who had tried to stop the first round of militia from rounding up the patients at the Planned Parenthood the first week of the insurrection. Up until that moment, he was always in charge. But then, one hard smack with the butt of a rifle and all order and understanding of his world left him; he just stood there as the men took the girls right past him and through the front door.

"Jeff," the witch said, pointing at Nicholas.

"Come again?" Nicholas asked, surprised.

"Jeff. That was his name," The witch said it like it should make perfect sense.

Nicholas stood and started to roll up his sleeves.

"Look, the money I sent her with. You were to get rid of it and you didn't, so I had to make someone else take care of it. You can hand it over or I can just have my men arrest you."

The Witch stood, matching Nicholas's icy stare. "Wait here," and the old witch walked into the back room returning with a stack of blue-colored bills. Nicholas reached out his hand and took them. He didn't object when the old woman placed his other hand over the bills and held them together, patting his hands like a proud grandmother.

"The next one I expect to be free," Nicholas said, pushing away and stuffing the money into his waistcoat. The room felt warm and Nicholas suddenly had the urge to drink something.

The witch smiled as she retreated to the back room. Nicholas wiped the new drops of sweat from his brow and drank the tea from the table. It tasted dreadful but it made his throat feel more open, and he could breathe easier now. He was still so thirsty though and he spotted the pitcher by the sink with cups already laid out. Nicholas poured a glass and emptied it immediately, only to repeat the cycle like a drunk pouring shots. The last sip tasted metallic, and Nicholas swallowed hard, hoping to end the bitterness.

His throat tightened with each swallow, however, so he looked for respite in the bottom of the empty pitcher until something caught his eye in the blackness of the deep container. Nicholas reached his hand in and felt something cold and soft, like a sea slug in the tide pool he would take the children to. Reaching in and gripping it tightly, Nicholas pulled out the gooey mess. He was disgusted as he marveled over this creature that looked like a big-headed seahorse. He brought it closer to his face, poking it with his other hand until the thing turned its bulbous head and squeaked out one word, "Dada."

Nicholas threw the thing in the air and stepped back in shock. The wet thud of the boneless body hitting the sink made him cringe. Its little body was crawling its way slowly toward Nicholas, and with each new scrape it said, "DADA."

Nicholas screamed and backed into the shelf separating the kitchen from the living room, its shelves lined with jars, the contents now stirring and pressing themselves against the glass of each one.

"DADA!" The cacophony was growing louder and soon Nicholas had to cover his ears to drown them out. The door to the tiny clinic wouldn't budge and Nicholas was not built to break it down. The things were crawling all over now. Some had slithered out of the jars and were snailing their way towards him, while others were pushing the large jars until they fell, smashing on the ground and freeing the things to crawl towards him. Some had limbs and even hair, but they all shared in the rising chorus with each movement closer to him.

Nicholas jumped as high as he could, crushing one into a paste when he landed. The ones he could not swat away burned through his fine silk clothing and embedded themselves into his skin, like a fly laying eggs. Nicholas crawled towards the bedroom door and pounded for the old witch to help. The things were upon him as he beat the wood, burrowing deeper into his flesh and filling him from the inside.

"Please! Get them out of me!" He screamed as his blood ran in hot streaks down the old door. "I'm sorry! I'm so sorry," he said, and in a last-ditch effort, Nicholas ran as hard as he could, shouldering the door, splintering it as he fell. It gave way to the darkness.

The old witch looked at the mess he had made and wondered what the drugs had made him see. Perhaps that was punishment enough. Then, she remembered the look on the girl's face and the hand she had not been able to put up in her defense. She emptied the entire syringe into Nicholas.

When he awoke, Nicholas was naked atop the rock formation in the creek behind the old witch's house. His head was pounding and his vision had just begun to clear when he noticed that staring back at him was Elise's head. He started to weep, noticing tiny arms circling all around him like an octopus made of infant parts.

"Elise, I'm so sorry," he cried toward the head, feeling the tiny fingernails rip into his legs.

The head started to rise, and from the limbs of the river-children it began to materialize into a bastardization of Elise's old form. The Old Witch sat in the house and sipped her tea, imagining Elise was somewhere with her baby, safe and happy. While it brought her little comfort knowing this would never be, the sound of Nicholas's maddening screams made the old Doctor smile.

ABOUT THE AUTHOR

Matthew Lutton is an up-and-coming author hailing from Newport Beach, California. Growing up in the sunny beach town, Matthew's imagination was sparked by the eerie and unexplainable happenings that would occur in the quiet corners of the city. He has always been fascinated with the horror genre and began writing his own stories as a way to explore his dark and twisted thoughts.

Matthew's debut anthology, "10 Drink Minimum" delves deep into the darkness of the human soul, exploring themes like fear, desperation, and madness. His tales are a unique blend of psychological horror, supernatural mystique, and visceral violence. Each story is crafted with precision, creating a world that is both hauntingly realistic and unforgettably surreal.

When he's not writing, Matthew loves to explore the California coastline and mountains, soaking up inspiration for his next tale of terror. He is a self-proclaimed film buff, especially when it comes to horror, and has a knack for spotting creative storytelling techniques that others may miss.

"10 Drink Minimum" has been met with critical acclaim, and has made its way onto many horror fans' must-read lists. Available now on Amazon, it showcases Matthew's unique storytelling voice and is a chilling journey into the depths of horror.

Printed in Great Britain
by Amazon